I0608006

OF HEAVEN AND HELLFIRE

MICHELLE ELLIOTT

1

BETH

Gilded rays of morning sun spread across the hills of Greenwich, England. Beth Dudley pulled the shawl tighter around her slight shoulders as the rickety wagon jostled down the cart path. Warm breath puffed from the old mare that pulled it. Autumn had arrived early, turning dew-covered fields into a landscape of glistening ice and the promise of colder days ahead.

"Work hard, Beth. Listen well, and Lord Charles and Lady Eleanore will be good to you, I'm sure of it," Peter said, giving the reins a slight flick.

Beth kept silent, knowing full well the old workhand with the weathered face had never stepped foot in Bodsworth Hall or strayed far from the fields of Abury Manor—the place that was no longer her home.

"You are young, clever, and a quick learner, too. I've seen you at the weave, and you bake bread as fine as the cook's buttered curd loaf—though don't tell her that." He chuckled and gave her a nudge with his elbow.

The words were intended to ease her anxiety and soothe the loss of everything she'd known in her short sixteen years, but they did not. Beth managed a small smile, but the sad, deep pools of her brown eyes said otherwise.

When told of her new position as a scullery maid for Lord and Lady Sheffield, Beth should have been happy and appreciative of the position offered. An orphan rarely had such a promising opportunity. Still, it did not change the sad fact that Lady Sarah Barrell, the grand lady of Abury Manor, was dead. The manor was no longer her home, and the only life Beth had known was gone.

Soon after Lady Sarah's passing, Queen Elizabeth had reclaimed the manor to do with it whatever she saw fit. Bestow it to another loyalist or keep it as her own and return it to her long list of estates.

Peter flicked the reins again, and the slumped-back horse broke into a trot. Not that Peter was in a rush to get to Bodsworth, since there was no home to return to. The current household at Abury was to be disbanded. They would sell all the familiar items and household goods to make way for a new owner who would bring their own tapestries, carved furniture, staff, and servants. Beth tried to convince herself of her good fortune in Lady Eleanore's need for kitchen help, and that she filled the lengthy list of requirements.

The mistress of Bodsworth had requested someone young yet experienced enough as to understand the importance of what was required in the kitchen and not to need an abundance of training or oversight. Although slight in build, Beth was strong. From hauling cast-iron pots to helping with the most intricate receipts, there was no chore in the manor kitchen she'd not made her own.

Margery, an undercook at Abury Manor, had taken a liking to Beth and, after her parent's death when she was a mere babe, raised and mentored her as if she were her own.

Having no memory of her parents made leaving the old cook all the harder. All Beth knew of her parents were their names, Beatrice and Arthur Dudley. Both had worked at the manor before passing from the sweating sickness. Whenever she'd asked Margery about them, the subject had been brushed away with a stern lecture about letting the past go, but Beth never could.

She stared out at the rambling hills and wondered if, perhaps, her stubborn, precocious nature reflected her father, and her slender, willowy frame and unruly, tawny curls came from her mother. Her eyes turned back to the path ahead as the answers escaped her.

The wagon jostled from a dip in the road, and Peter cursed the rugged trail under his breath.

Beth watched a farmer at a passing cottage carry a grain sack into a crooked barn. A young boy scurried behind him with a pail, and she tried to imagine living with her own family, together and whole. No one knew that, at night, alone and sullen, she often whispered her parents' names, as if conjuring them with a spell. Come morning, faced with the truth, she'd remind herself of her good fortune to be taken in by Lady Sarah and Margery.

Beth was bright and determined. She learned to braise lamb, roast beef, and bake fruit pies and pastries. Peter was right about baking bread, too. Beth also wove fabric and sewed and kept a proper kitchen garden. She thought that if anything, Lady Eleanore was the fortunate one to have her.

"I know little about the place or the people," Margery had said to Beth after Lady Eleanore agreed to take her on. "But it's a far better fate than most of us here face—starting all over again and finding our way." She stared at Beth's forlorn face. "All will be well," she'd said briskly, patting Beth's hand. "I'm sure of it." Marge had feigned a smile and laid a handful of straw over the basket of kitchenware ready to be loaded into the wagon.

Beth had stayed quiet, not wanting to appear ungrateful.

"Don't look so gloomy, girl. It won't change the situation. It's time for resilience. Now is the time to be strong," Margery had continued. Her voice had broken as she wiped her dewy eyes with a stained apron.

Tears filled Beth's eyes as she remembered wrapping her arms around the woman's thick waist. "I will make you proud," she had promised, swallowing her tears, wondering if she would ever see the sweet woman again.

To Beth's good fortune, Lady Sarah had also expressed a fondness for her and generously provided her with a modest education and instruction in courtly manners. Her husband, Lord Thomas, had died young, leaving her ladyship childless and alone. Margery had little to say about Thomas, only that he had been a hard, cruel man, more concerned with hunting and hawking than domestic life. The man had also been a staunch supporter of Queen Elizabeth and the Reformation, although Beth was unsure what that meant. Marge's dour face had made Beth decide that the matter was best left alone, despite her lingering questions.

Yet, Beth remembered long afternoons in the library after Lady Sarah called for her once the day's work was done. The older woman's faded blue eyes had danced with delight, and the age lines deepened with merriment as Beth had recited Shakespearean stanzas from memory. Under Lady Sarah's guidance, Beth had learned to read and write and explored music and the arts, finding solace in the gentle melodies of the harpsichord.

"You're a clever girl," Lady Sarah would say wistfully, her gaze lingering on the fields beyond the paned glass. Anyone would be proud to call you daughter."

Beth's heart would swell with pride like a river overflowing its banks. She'd longed to wrap her arms around the woman who treated her so well, as she'd often had with Margery, but etiquette and fear held her back, restraining the affection she'd yearned to express. Those moments had brought her a bittersweet melancholy. Lady Sarah had no children of her own and dedicated herself to the upkeep of Abury Manor and the reputation of the Barrell name. She had been a lost and lonely caretaker until Beth came along, and it had been only natural for her to take a young orphan under her wing, offering guidance and kindness in a world often devoid of both.

Although it had been several weeks since her passing, Lady Sarah's death haunted her still.

"She's gone," Margery had said on the morning they'd found the old woman cold and lifeless in bed.

"Gone?" The word had been strange on Beth's tongue, as if Lady Sarah had simply disappeared into the air like steam from a kettle. Pain had overwhelmed her, ripping up the love in her heart by the roots, leaving a hollow, bitter void.

As the wagon rumbled along, Beth pushed away the memories, good and bad, no longer wishing to revisit the past. Yet, the past trailed behind her, like the winding road on which she traveled.

"It shouldn't be much longer now," Peter said. "We'll stop soon for some of the bread Marge packed for us."

Beth had nothing left of Abury Manor except for a small trunk of clothes and Margery's sourdough tightly wrapped in linen. Although her stomach rumbled with hunger, she decided to delay eating her share of the tasty bread, wanting to savor her last memory of Marge.

Pounding hooves coming rapidly behind them interrupted her thoughts. The ground shook under the thunderous weight and speed.

"Make way!" a voice shouted, but the old bay was not used to such commotion. With a hard buck from the horse, their hay wagon traveled aimlessly down the road, making it impossible to pass.

Peter swore under his breath and yanked the reins hard to the left, barely pulling the confused nag and the wagon off the path to avoid a collision.

Six men, grouped two by two, drew to a halt beside them. Four were soldiers donning the queen's colors. One man in front wore a long black robe with a silver cross embroidered on the back. A cleric's cap covered his head. The man next to him wore a crimson doublet and a breastplate with a cross made of jewels in the center. The horses reared and danced in place.

The man with the breastplate removed his leather riding gloves, dismounted from the saddle, and approached. "Did you not see us? How dare you not move aside for the queen's retinue!" His ginger beard did little to hide his square, clenched jaw, and his wild, coal-black eyes flashed with anger.

Peter doffed his cap and said, "We saw you alright, but this old nag hasn't left a hayfield in twenty years. Not used to seeing steeds twice her size, I guess. Got spooked, is all. Didn't mean any disrespect, sir."

"Where are you headed?" the elderly cleric asked. Despite his age, he sat tall in the saddle. His face was pale and narrow, with a hooked nose and close-set eyes that pierced like arrows. Something about his eyes made Beth look away.

"Bodsworth Hall," Peter replied, motioning at Beth. I'm delivering the girl here to Lady Eleanore. She is under her employ."

The man turned his cool gaze on Beth. "Is this true?"

Beth nodded. "It is," she replied, looking down at her hands.

"Come along, Sir Bayne," the old cleric told his counterpart. "There's no reason to linger and waste time while heretics hide amongst us."

The man beside the cleric grunted and abruptly turned to go, but just as quickly, he swung around and struck Peter across the cheek with his riding gloves. Blood trickled from Peter's nose.

Beth's hands flew to her mouth, stifling the yelp that escaped her.

"That's a lesson in attentiveness," the man said, eyeing the bread between them. He reached over, snatched the loaf, and mounted his horse. "And this? This is for our midday meal." He stuffed the loaf into his saddle pouch, and the men wheeled their horses around and galloped away.

Anger rose in Beth's throat, but she resisted the urge to shout after them. She touched Peter's arm. "Are you alright?"

Peter snorted, wiping the blood on his sleeve. "Aye, I'll be fine. Been in tavern brawls worse than that."

Beth had never witnessed such brutality before, especially against someone as kind and harmless as Peter. It left her shaken and bewildered.

"Who were those men?" she asked.

"Priest hunters, I reckon."

"Priest hunters? I've never heard of such men."

"You wouldn't. The battle of wills and religion began long ago. You were but a wee babe when Queen Mary's bloody reign began. Looks like her sister, Elizabeth, means to outdo her."

"I don't understand."

Peter shifted uncomfortably, debating whether to explain a subject difficult to make sense of.

"You were raised a Protestant," he said hesitantly.

"Of course, it is the law and religion of the land," Beth replied matter-of-factly.

"But not always. Before Elizabeth, when her half-sister Queen Mary reigned, everyone was Catholic. Mary brought back her childhood faith as the English religion again. She snuffed out all remnants of the Protestants, and God again became head of the church." He paused and looked away as if not wanting to continue, but said, "It was akin to a cleansing, and a horrible one. Mary put to the stake all who refused to convert and tortured many others." He made the sign of the cross.

Beth crossed herself, too. "How awful!"

"Now, Her Majesty wants the Protestant faith restored."

"For what purpose?" Beth asked, wondering why a queen as beloved as Elizabeth would want to divide her people.

"Men whisper in the alehouses that she is easily led by the Reformers around her. They claim a Catholic rebellion is near. She fears an uprising." He surveyed the surrounding hills as if spies hid among the trees. "Do you know what kings and queens hold dearer than God?"

"No," Beth answered.

Peter leaned in closer. "Loyal subjects. Now that Catholic loyalty is under question, the middle path walked by all grows narrower every day."

Beth regretted her curiosity about the priest hunters. How did she not know such things? Lady Sarah's thorough instruction had been most welcome, and Beth had been an ardent student. Her lessons had included all the monarchs, including King Henry VIII and his unfortunate wives, Anne Boleyn and Catherine Howard, who lost their heads on the block.

Why did Lady Sarah omit that dark past from her studies? It had never occurred to Beth to question religion. Church teachings and the queen's authority were absolute—fixed as a mother's love or the sinking sun at day's end. Yet, confronted with the harsh realities of persecution, Beth wondered about loyalty and the very nature of right and wrong.

"Queen Elizabeth's men, bands of royal rogues, came for the books first—Bibles, hymnals, things of that sort," Peter continued. "When that wasn't enough, they condemned and banned Mass. Now they've come for the priests. Jesuits especially, although I'm not sure why. Are not all men of the cloth the same?" Something in his voice carried a hint of sadness, a memory perhaps, that still pained him.

"Are you one of them? . . . Catholic, I mean," Beth asked softly.

Peter flicked the reins and stared at the road ahead. "I am who they say I am. Nothing more."

At that moment, Beth understood the queen's men had stolen more than bread.

Bodsworth Hall was an enormous manor house served by the village of Surrey. Surrounded by a moat, its brick three-story facade was as imposing as it was beautiful. Eight chimneys stood sentry on the slate-covered roof. The main building was the largest, with two more minor additions on either side.

The grand receiving hall served both dining and entertaining. The rest of the first floor boasted lavish drawing rooms, a library, a den, a music room, and many other chambers devoted to recreation. Family chambers were on the second floor, and servants' quarters occupied the third. Beth had arrived over a week ago and had yet to meet Lady Eleanore.

Much like the kitchen at Abury the days began early, but without Marge and the staff's easy banter, Beth felt a sense of duty instead of the usual camaraderie. She tried to put the incident on the road aside, deciding to keep it to herself. Who was there to tell? She found herself immersed in a world of strangers. There was nothing she could do but learn her place, adapt and endure. She hoped eventually to learn about Peter's fate and Marge's, too, wishing them a more fortunate lot. The violent slap Peter had endured played over in her mind, and the tale of the priest hunters lingered. Her unsettled sleep kept her tossing and turning in the bed she shared with eighteen-year-old Kat, another scullery maid.

At Abury, Beth had shared a room over the granary with an older maid. The woman had weathered skin, and her clothes smelled of harvested wheat. She threshed and sacked grain during the day, and the two saw little of each other except during the evening when they were both too tired for anything but simple pleasantries before retiring for the night. Beth was initially excited about the possibility of rooming with another scullery maid her age, but the excitement faded quickly.

Kat was slim, with long, unkempt curls that framed a narrow face. She was a peasant girl from the village and, like most servants, worked for the Sheffields to help pay the rent her family owed the manor house to farm the village fields. Kat was tasked with training Beth and lorded it over her as if she were her superior. Worse still, Beth quickly realized Kat was not interested in making friends, as Kat made it clear that Beth was not welcome.

"The chair and footstool are mine. So is the pillow. Find your own," Kat had told Beth early on.

The days that followed had been no better. Kat seemed to relish proving her authority.

On one occasion, Beth had caught Kat rummaging through her trunk.

"What are you doing?" Beth demanded, startled by the intrusion.

"Searching for anything worth keeping," Kat said with a smug grin.

"Don't touch my things!" Beth had snapped, her cheeks flushed with anger. "I'm warning you!"

Kat had thrown her head back and laughed. "Warning *me*? You are nothing but an annoying flea to be swatted away. You best remember that." She'd slammed the trunk shut with a smirk. "No worries. Nothing worth keeping in there."

Beth had let the comment go but not the anger and vowed to follow through on her warning.

A few days after the incident, Beth rose as she did each morning and pulled on her linen shift. She carefully spiral-laced the woolen kirtle, tugging the laces tight. She pinned her flaxen waves together and tucked them under her wimple. Closing the bedchamber door softly behind her, she made her way to the servants' hall. Her day began with hard cheese, sourdough—and a heavy heart. As she chewed the stale loaf, her thoughts turned, as they often did, to Marge.

After finding her way to the main kitchen, Beth had barely tied her apron when Kat thrust a basket of root vegetables into her arms and ordered her to peel them. Not accustomed to such gruffness, a flush rose to Beth's cheeks, but she picked up a paring knife and reached for a turnip.

"Wash them first!" Kat scolded and sighed, pointing at the water bucket. "I was told you had *some* training."

Beth bristled, put the blade down, and minded her tongue. The kitchen at Bodsworth was far different from what she was used to. Mistakes, missteps, and failures were called out. There were no more gentle lessons or guidance to be had. She would have to take things as they came and find her way.

The complexity of the Bodsworth kitchen was overwhelming. Two enormous fireplaces stood at either end, one for meat and the other for baked goods and cooking. Every cast iron pot and pan imaginable hung from massive metal arms raised and lowered by a pulley when needed. A pantry dedicated to trenchers, ewers, silver cutlery, and priceless serving dishes acted as an entryway to the rest of the house, and a backdoor led to the kitchen gardens, farmyard, carriage house, and stables.

Everyone answered to Benjamin Eldridge, the master cook. As round as he was tall, Benjamin wobbled about the kitchen wearing a chef's woolen beret, overseeing the elaborate meals and intricate receipts as if he were lord of the manor.

The undercook, Annie, was in charge of the lesser-important staff. She was also stout, but short and of middle age, her cheeks permanently reddened from years spent over hot pots. She had said little to Beth on her arrival, just given her a welcoming nod, too distracted by an upcoming feast.

"Fetch me some salt, Kat, and be quick about it. The bread is mangled again." Annie waved a floured hand at the girl and shook her head in disgust. "I'll have to start again. You'd think I could manage simple bread after twenty years in the kitchen," she mumbled to no one in particular.

Beth moved closer to the woman, close enough to see the mound of flattened dough on the board. "The yeast is dead," she said quietly.

"What do you know of bread-making, girl?" Annie scoffed, and her voice grew louder. "The new maid thinks herself a royal baker!"

Beth lowered her eyes. "I know more sugar is better than too much salt, and beer yeast dies much sooner if stored too close to heat," she answered, sure of the skills imparted by Marge.

As Kat returned with the salt, Annie scooped up the dough and flung it into the scrap bucket. "Never mind that," she told Kat. "Go see the alewife and bring back more brewer's yeast."

Kat looked at both of them. Her eyes narrowed as she pointed at Beth. "Make her go. There are chores to be done, and with the pace this wench moves, how will they ever get done?"

"Don't back-talk me!" Annie seethed. "Beth here will stay and help bake the bread."

Before Kat uttered another word, her eyes widened in alarm. Beth turned to see what had startled the girl. In the pantry doorway stood Lady Eleanore. Beth gasped at her ladyship's unannounced arrival. The noblewoman was both shapely and statuesque, and her maroon satin gown accentuated her slender waist and ivory complexion. A net of pearls adorned her amber hair, which was woven into an elaborate braid. Large periwinkle eyes set in her angular face radiated a curiosity that was neither kind nor harsh.

"I beg your pardon, my lady," Annie said with a deep curtsy, and all the kitchen staff followed.

"Good morning," Lady Eleanore said, ignoring the discord. "Where is Master Eldridge?

"In the Orangerie, my lady, seeing about the pineapples and lemons for the fruit platters," Annie answered.

Lady Eleanore's frown imparted her dismay at the master cook's absence. She surveyed the disarray on the wooden preparation tables. "I trust things are moving along for our guests and the banquet dinner?"

Annie scrambled for a wrinkled paper. "Yes, my lady. Roasted duck, pickled vegetables, lamb stew, mushroom pasty, cherry pottage, and honey cakes."

"Very good. Bring four barrels of ale from the cellar and two of the wine," Lady Eleanore said, pleased with the offering, then turned her attention to Beth. "And this is our new scullery maid?"

Beth curtsied again. "Yes, my lady."

"Come to my chamber when your workday is done."

2

GARETH

Before working at Bodsworth Hall, Gareth Montgomery had been an apprentice at the village blacksmith shop owned by his father, George.

Taught the art of swinging hammers and forging metal at the tender age of ten, Gareth liked blacksmithing as much as emptying piss pots and wasting Sunday mornings at church. Much to his father's dismay, Gareth had never hidden his loathing of the trade, trudging behind the rugged man like a fattened calf trailing a butcher.

Closed up in the smith shed with the threat of flying shrapnel and seared flesh, Gareth had longed for fields of yellow wheat, neat pea rows, and fat pigs hanging in the smokehouse—a tenant farm of his own. Yet, every hammer he'd swung felt like another blow to that dream, and the suffocating heat of the forge mirrored his father's smothering expectations.

George Montgomery had dreams of his own. He never failed to remind Gareth that the smithy would one day be his, just as it had passed from father to son before. But when Gareth dared speak of the future, George's disapproving glance cut sharper than any blade they forged.

When Gareth was scarcely ten years old, the tariffs owed to the manor became too much for the blacksmith shop. In danger of losing the fields that fed the family, the Montgomerys—not unlike many other Surrey families with children and bills to pay—had reluctantly offered Gareth to Bodsworth to bridge the gap by working in the stables, becoming a spit boy, and perhaps, with any luck, advancing as a page or chamber servant.

When told of his new lot, Gareth had hidden his joy as his mother had hidden her sorrow, since he was the first child to leave the homestead. With a fierce embrace and tearful eyes, she handed him his meager belongings, knowing his task was vital to the family's survival.

Seven years later, as Gareth rubbed tanning oil into Lord Charles' favorite saddle, his dream of farming felt very far away. Along with his stable duties, he served as a spit-turner and errand boy, which, on most days, was a pleasant change from the stern manner of the stable master. Despite the challenges, Gareth found solace in the camaraderie of the other stable lads and the kitchen servants, a warmth that helped him endure his daily work.

Gareth looked up from his task, hearing footsteps approach. The kitchen maid, Kat, appeared in the stable doorway swinging a wire basket. Her usual unruly hair was tucked away, and her lip curled ever so slightly, as if holding back a secret.

"Annie sent me for eggs from the coop." She smiled brightly. "Care to help? One rooster is quite hateful and pecks my ankles." She lifted her dress to expose her stocking-covered calf.

Gareth shook his head, looking back down at the saddle seat. Kat was nice enough, but always had an excuse to come to the stable. He had always resisted the ways of women. Not that he didn't care for them. Plenty of pretty village girls and manor maids looked upon him with coy eyes and teasing smiles. He grinned politely at their advances, but his dream kept him disciplined and well-focused; besides, becoming a husband and managing a family would only make life more complicated, and life was already slipping by like the rush of a swollen river. He had to admit, though, lying on his pallet alone in the cold stable at night, thoughts of a girl with soft curves and a warm embrace were never far from his mind.

"Lord Charles wants all the tack cleaned and ready for the guest's arrival," he said, grateful for the task.

"I scrounged some scraps for Fritz," she answered, ignoring his excuse. She pulled a rag filled with pork fat from her apron pocket and looked around. "Where is the little mutt?"

"With the shepherd herding sheep from the high pasture. Leave the scraps if you like. I'll see he gets them," Gareth replied without looking up. "I'm sure he'll be hungry when he returns," he added, not wanting to sound ungrateful.

"All this fuss over a carpenter," Kat suddenly said, plopping down on a hay bale beside him. "I don't understand why everyone must make such a fuss. I mean, giving a banquet for someone like that? He's no nobleman. Lady Eleanore even employed a new scullery maid. I wonder about that, too. We were fine without her. Now, I'm obliged to follow her around and fix her mistakes like a mother hen."

Gareth brushed his dark bangs aside and focused on bringing the lackluster saddle skirt to a sheen, wishing Kat would get on with her egg gathering. "I wish I had an answer, Kat. All I know is that Master Owen has a reputation all over England for his trade," he said, struggling to converse with so many tasks to get done.

Kat replied with a heavy sigh and looked around. "Don't know how you can stand this stinking barn. Working in the stables must be quite a bore. I much prefer it when you help in the kitchen."

"I go where I'm told," Gareth said, swiping more tallow onto his rag, "but someday, I'll leave here. Have a tenant farm of my own. My fate will be my own." His words carried a quiet determination, a resolve that refused to be dampened by the laughter that followed.

"Go on with you!" Kat cried. "A farm? Are you mad?" She tossed her head back, cackling at the notion. "We're servants and that's all we'll ever be."

Gareth bristled and regretted confiding in her about his dream. Kat was not the first to doubt his aspirations. The memory of his father's snide remarks and teasing had only made Gareth more persistent over the years.

"You'll see," Gareth told her angrily. "Someday, when you wake and find me gone, you'll know you were wrong, just like my father is wrong, too!"

Kat's amber eyes softened, and so did her tone. "Forgive me. I say silly things. Ask Cook. I'm always prattling on and making jokes."

Gareth rubbed the leather harder under the weight of her stare.

"Of course, you'll be a fine farmer someday. The best," she added gently. "You could take me with you, perhaps. I could help harvest the fields, tend the garden, and keep a tidy kitchen."

Gareth's temper flared and he shook his head forcefully. "No," he said. "It's my dream and mine alone. I refuse to have a woman, *any* woman, tag along like a wagon tethered behind me."

Kat's eyes narrowed. "You think yourself my better? Is that it?"

Gareth lifted the saddle and slung it over his shoulder, carrying it down the stable aisle to the wooden saddle benches.

Kat followed, tugging at his arm. "Answer me!"

At that moment, the vast barn doors pulled open, and the other stable lads filed in, each leading Lord Charles's most prized geldings and mares after their morning exercise. Gareth turned to help lead them to their stalls, but found Kat blocking his path, refusing to move.

"Kat, please," he said, attempting to hurry around her. "I meant no offense. I must get to my work."

But his words were unconvincing, and Kat blocked his path again.

"You'll draw the master's attention!" Gareth seethed. "Let me pass!"

He was correct. Moments later, the stable master, Edmund Telford, stormed into the barn. The man was a towering figure with a presence that commanded respect and, at times, fear. His broad shoulders and muscular build were a testament to years of hard labor, and his calloused and scarred hands spoke of countless hours spent handling unruly horses and maintaining the stables.

"Where is Gareth?" Telford growled. "Why aren't the feed troughs filled, and the hay spread?" His steely eyes searched about.

Gareth's voice lowered with a beseeching plea. "Please, Kat! I am not your better. We are friends! We always have been and always will be! I must do my duty now! Let me pass!"

Gareth's imploring and desperate state worked its charm on Kat, and she stepped aside with an air of importance.

Gareth hurried past with relief, but he heard Kat call after him before she slipped out a side door.

"We may be friends, Gareth Montgomery, but someday we shall be more. Mark my words. We shall be more!"

Gareth felt under his feather mattress, ensuring the small sack of coins remained hidden. There wasn't much there—perhaps a dozen groats squirreled away from the fish he pinched from the river and sold to travelers on the road. Poaching was illegal. The river trout belonged to Lord Charles and, if caught by the warden, meant a one-way trip to the gallows, but there was no other way to make the coin needed to escape the manor.

Satisfied the pouch was safe, he rolled onto his back and pulled the bedclothes back over him, ready for sleep. Fritz lay curled at the pallet foot, already asleep with a belly full of Kat's scraps. Yet sleep did not come to Gareth as

Thomas, his friend, suddenly plopped beside him with a flagon of ale.

"Here," Thomas said with a cheeky grin, handing him the leather pouch. "Drink."

Gareth sat up and took a long draught. "Where did you get this?"

Although it was late, Thomas' company was welcome after the tongue-lashing he suffered from Master Telford.

"The alewife's daughter gave it to me. Don't ask me what I gave her in return," Thomas said with a wink and took another draught himself.

Thomas was tall and wiry but strong as a field horse, and Gareth always marveled at the way he tossed the heavy bales up to the loft as if they were weightless.

Gareth grinned and shook his head. "I'm sure the trade was fair."

"You had a rough go of it today," Thomas said, wiping his mouth on his sleeve.

"There are days I wish my duty was in the kitchen instead of the barn, for sure."

Thomas clapped him on the back. "Are you sure it has nothing to do with the girl I saw sidle out the back door?"

Gareth gave him a playful shove, the warm rush of ale taking effect. "No. As usual, Kat was an unwelcome distraction. Because of her, Telford caught me slacking."

"Kat from the kitchen? She comes around a lot, I noticed," Thomas said, his eyes twinkling with mischief.

"She's always eager to pawn her chores off on me," Gareth replied. "This time it was egg-gathering." He rolled his eyes.

"Seems she's got more than eggs on her mind."

Gareth sighed, feeling the weight of the day pressing down on him. "She's looking for someone to tease, is all. I can't afford to be distracted."

Thomas nodded, understanding his friend's serious tone. "You've got a good head on your shoulders, and I admire your goals, Gareth. But don't let them blind you to the present. Sometimes, it's the moments we least expect that shape our future."

Gareth looked at his friend. There was truth in his words, but the yearning for his own land, his own tenant farm, was a fire that burned too brightly to ignore.

"I'll remember that," he said, taking another gulp of ale. "But for now, I must stay on track. My dream is all I've got."

Thomas raised the flagon in a mock salute. "To your dream, then. May it come true sooner than you think."

3

BETH

Beth gently rapped on the carved door that led to Lady Eleanore's second-floor den and waited for permission to enter.

She had only left the kitchen a few times to sweep the cold embers from the library and music room fireplaces and refill the tinderboxes. These tasks gave her a better idea of the manor's layout, and she quickly memorized how to maneuver the many hallways and staircases. The den was connected to Lady Eleanore's bedchamber, and the outer chambers and wardrobes shared the same hallway. Lord Charles's chamber had a similar floor plan directly down the hall.

On her way to the music room, Beth had passed Lord Charles. Slightly older than Eleanore, Charles presented a distinguished air with a neatly trimmed beard and determined face. Beth had made herself inconspicuous by pressing against the wall to make way, but he'd paused as he'd passed, and she'd felt his cool glance upon her.

Beth heard a voice commanding her to come in, and she entered the room. Lady Eleanore sat on a chaise in the center of the spacious den. Her long-sleeved gown of emerald satin and white lace complemented her flawless complexion. A writing desk and several bookcases lined one wall. Across the room was an armoire and a few sizable trunks. Woven tapestries, hung by long iron rods, covered the walls, and lit tapers flickered a muted glow of red and golden hues around the room.

"Are you getting along well enough?" her mistress asked, looking her over.

Beth curtsied low as Lady Sarah had taught her. "Yes, my lady. Quite well," she replied, shamefully aware of the gray soot smeared across her white apron.

"I'm glad. I'm sure it is odd being a stranger in new surroundings, away from all that is familiar."

Her tone was sympathetic, and Beth wondered if she was genuinely concerned with her well-being or merely took pity on her current state.

"I have been made welcome," Beth said, unsure of how to answer.

"Your former cook mentioned you have courtly training, including music and recitation. You also have some culinary knowledge and are familiar with the needle. She also praised your trustworthiness among your many talents."

Beth watched as Eleanore stood and approached the window. She pressed her long, slender fingers against the diamond-shaped panes as if to ward off the late autumn chill.

"Lady Barrell imparted this worldly and courtly knowledge?" Eleanore asked.

Beth nodded. "Lady Sarah and the cook Margery were fond of me. I was fortunate despite being an orphan."

"What of piety?" Lady Eleanore asked, her voice tight. "Did Lady Sarah's training include that of godly pursuits?"

The question caught Beth off guard. She had never considered herself devout; of that, she was certain. The Protestant service left her restless. The Bible readings were dense and difficult to understand. In truth, Beth cared more about living a decent, honest life than a pious one. Still, she had attended church services dutifully along with the Abury household, as the law demanded. "Yes, my lady," she answered.

"Many held the widow Barrell in high esteem, particularly following Lord Barrell's death—I did not," her new mistress replied, her voice carrying a sharp edge. "I visited Abury Manor as a child and remember it well. Too well," she added with a wry smile.

Eleanore's stern tone and disapproving words against Lady Sarah shocked Beth, but she was quick to hide any hint of feelings from her face and defensiveness from her tone as she said, "My learned upbringing is due to her kindness."

"What of your parents?"

Beth shifted uncomfortably, not having expected such intense questioning. "I was told both succumbed to the sweating sickness. My grandparents, as well."

Lady Eleanore abruptly turned to her. "Who told you that?" she snapped.

Beth lowered her head, still confused by the woman's sudden turn. "Cook and Lady Sarah. Their benevolence towards me was unending."

"Ah, yes, benevolence . . ." Eleanore mused. She was silent for a moment, then said more calmly, "It must be peculiar knowing both worlds, the one of courtly ways and the other of servitude."

Beth felt inclined to tell Lady Eleanore that she did not have an affinity for either world and longed to find the place where she belonged, if such a place existed. Instead, she answered, "That is true, my lady."

"The cook also wrote that you weave, sew, and crochet." Lady Eleanore moved to a trunk and lifted the cover. "Consider this a test to determine if the boasts about you are true. You will mend these dresses for me." She pulled out two neatly folded gowns and handed them to Beth, along with a sewing basket. "You shall alter the sleeves two inches on the red gown and close the gap in the neckline on the gray. They need to be ready for the upcoming banquet. I will choose between the two once they are ready. Can you manage that?"

"Of course," Beth said, curtsying once more, careful not to let the fabric slip from her grasp.

She had often mended Lady Sarah's gowns and garments, marveling at the intricate beadwork, vibrant colors, and butter-soft fabrics.

The thought of having to prove herself was unsettling, and something about Lady Eleanore's abruptness toward Lady Sarah brought an uneasiness. There was something cold beneath her beauty, something calculating.

"Two significant guests shall arrive in two days' time, as I'm sure you've gathered from the furor in the kitchen," Lady Eleanore said, sounding amused. "For now, you shall remain there and assist the cook, but I will call on you occasionally for special tasks and to perform errands for our guests."

"Of course, it would be my honor," Beth replied earnestly, her arms full of gowns she had only dreamt of ever wearing. She curtsied and turned to leave.

"And Beth," Lady Eleanore said.

"Yes, my lady."

"Make sure the bread is not ruined."

The next day, Beth rushed through her kitchen work, eager to inspect Lady Eleanore's gowns and begin alterations. Kat curiously noted Beth's faster pace while prepping vegetables.

Although she was grateful for Lady Sarah and Margery's tutelage, sewing was not one of her strengths. She remembered the endless hours tearing out crooked hems and faulty seams.

"What of those dresses the mistress gave you?" Kat asked.

"Just gowns that need mending," Beth answered.

The girls spoke in low voices as they shelled peas. Annie didn't tolerate frivolous talk in her kitchen and was more irritable than usual with guests arriving on the morrow.

"The manor seamstresses do that," Kat sniffed.

Beth thought it best not to tell Kat about the test put forth to her. The girl was already a thorn in her side, so she came up with a lie.

"Lady Eleanore wishes me to alter them because the head seamstress has taken ill, and she needs to choose a gown for the banquet. I learned the craft of sewing at Abury Manor."

Kat's eyes widened in disbelief. "Seamstress! For the mistress? But whatever for? There are under seamstresses for that," she persisted.

"Who am I to question our lady's command?" Beth replied, although she, too, realized how ridiculous it sounded.

Kat held the paring knife as if to cut some imaginary delicacy. "I have a brilliant idea. You be the new seamstress while I attend a feast at Hampton Court," she teased, laughing loudly this time.

"More work and less chatter, girls! The peas will not shell themselves!" the cook scolded from across the kitchen.

"Don't believe me. I don't care," Beth said under her breath, her tone unwavering.

Kat's smirk faded slightly at Beth's steady reply, but before she could respond, a young man burst through the back door, struggling with a barrel.

Dressed in a linen groomsman shirt, he was of medium height and broad through the shoulders and chest with a slim figure that narrowed at the waist. A mop of chestnut curls that brushed his shoulders framed his rugged, bronzed face. Beth watched as he waited for Annie's order.

"Put it over there," Annie finally said, waving to an empty corner. "Be quick about it. Several more need to be brought from the cellar."

Annie strode into the pantry, mumbling about a larger stew pot as the young man swiftly rolled the barrel into place.

Before Beth and Kat could resume their work, a small, scruffy dog with a gray spotted coat and pointed ears darted through the open door. Finding the scrap bucket beside them, the dog buried its head in the empty pea pods and quickly snapped them up.

"Cook will tan your hide, Gareth!" Kat scolded. "She warned you about letting Fritz in the kitchen!"

"Well, I couldn't very well shut the door with a barrel of ale in my arms!" he shot back. "Loads of help you were!"

Kat scooped up the bucket and put it on the table. After a few strokes across the dog's wiry fur, she shooed Fritz out the door and secured it. Kat's smile at Gareth hinted to Beth that she would have done more than shut the door for him.

Cook returned from the pantry, pale and shaken. "They're here!" she cried, assessing the unfinished business in the kitchen.

"Who?" Kat asked.

Annie threw her hands up in frustration. "The guests! They're a day early! I heard the chatter in the great hall. Master Owen and his apprentice are off to their quarters as we speak!"

The kitchen fell silent as Master Benjamin barged through the back door. His fat cheeks were missing their usual rosy hue as his piggish eyes landed on Annie.

"The guests are here!" he shouted at the poor woman.

"I am aware, sir," she said, her voice wavering.

"You didn't tell me!"

"I was just informed, sir, same as you."

The master cook grunted, and his angry eyes scanned the kitchen staff. "No time to stand about! Get to work!" he barked, and the servants scurried about, panicked.

Beth moved to Annie, who appeared wan and ready to collapse.

"It's not your fault," she soothed and guided the woman into the pantry, away from the man's rage.

Yet, Annie's eyes filled with tears as she made her way to a nearby stool. "Of course, it's my fault. I am the manor undercook. I should have known this situation could arise."

Beth placed a comforting hand on her shoulder. "Master Eldridge should have known as well. His oversight is clearly lacking," Beth told her, remembering the orderly Abury kitchen. "Tell us what needs to be done. All will be made right again."

Annie looked up at Beth with doubtful eyes. "Let's pray it will."

The rest of the day was a blur of chaos. A newly motivated Annie took command of her staff. Pots simmered, sauces thickened, and rich cuts of meat sizzled over the spit. Enticing aromas wafted about the kitchen, and the staff worked with meticulous care, wanting to satisfy and redeem their mistress.

Beth was tasked with polishing the ewers and cutlery by applying a mixture of olive oil and lemon. She paused from her work when Gareth, the lad with the dog, appeared rolling another large barrel to a nearby wall. He set the heavy drum upright next to the others, then stopped. Beth hastily lowered her eyes, hoping he had not seen her watching him.

After a long moment, he said, "You're the new kitchen maid."

Beth nodded. "I am. I arrived from Abury Manor a short time ago." She gazed at him with curious eyes, unsure of his position. "You dress as a stable hand, yet you serve in the kitchen."

His hazel eyes were penetrating as he reached for a shiny fork and held it up to the light. "That's right. I am also a spit boy, messenger, field hand, and whatever Annie and Master Telford ask of me. I do everything except what I want to do," he added, his tone sharp, and tossed the fork back into the crate.

Beth bristled at the treatment of the manor's fine cutlery. "Careful! You'll be blamed for dents and scratches, not me!" she scolded, wishing he would let her alone.

His lips curled into a teasing grin. "From what I hear, it's you who bumbles about making mistakes."

Beth's cheeks burned. "That's not true! Who would say such a thing?" The moment the words left her mouth, she remembered Kat. Of course, it was Kat. "Aren't you needed in the stable?" she spat. "I'm sure the guest's horses need attention."

"Two riders leave little to be done. It's not as if they arrived with a grand entourage," he answered with an eye roll. "Telford told me to go where I'm needed most. It's easy to pick a nice, warm kitchen over a cold livery." He reached for a broom and swept the dirt dragged in by the barrel.

Beth swallowed the lump rising in her throat. The gentle voice of Marge echoed in her head, reminding her to be resilient and strong, and that all would be well. Yet, nothing felt right. She felt disconnected and adrift. It was clear she would never have a friend at Bodsworth, and she promised herself to be ever vigilant in the future against lies and rumors spread by Kat.

As the afternoon passed, Beth completed her task in silence, ignoring Gareth, who quietly filled the wood boxes and carried in baskets of root vegetables. She gathered the crate to present to Annie, but before she rose from the worktable, Gareth slid down on the bench across from her.

"Forgive me," he said in a low, serious voice. "I shouldn't have made merry at your expense. You're a stranger here.

It's not easy. I know." His eyes held a steady gaze. "I was a stranger once, too."

Beth nodded, but did not answer, not trusting the sincerity in his voice. An uncomfortable silence settled between them, and she thought it best to change the subject. "These guests who arrived must be quite important," she said.

Gareth nodded. "Nicholas Owen is a master builder and well-known carpenter. He's to work on the east wing library."

"Will they be here long?"

Gareth shrugged and said, "A good while, I'd wager. The spring rains damaged both the walls and the floor. It's no small task to repair them. I'm surprised it hasn't given way with the weight of all the books."

Annie approached from behind, catching them off-guard. She peered into the cutlery box, pleased with what she found. "We may have a banquet after all," she said to Beth, then turned to Gareth. "You'll go to the village on Sunday to fetch the items Master Owen requested." She nodded at Beth. "She'll go, as well, to see nothing is forgotten."

"I don't need help, mistress," Gareth replied abruptly. "I've run errands to the village many times with no trouble."

Annie's stare turned hard. "And that's the way we'll keep it. Can't afford any more mishaps or mistakes. Master

Owen's list is long—many odds and ends needed to get his work started," she said, before turning to go.

Lady Eleanore appeared a short time later and was pleased with what she found. The feast was laid out, and everything was as she expected. Platters overflowed with food ready to be served.

"All appears to be in order," Lady Eleanore said to Annie, whose plump cheeks turned a deeper shade of red as she beamed and accepted the praise on Master Benjamin's behalf, as he was with the wine keeper, a man who did more drinking than tasting.

Eleanore turned to Beth. "My gowns are prepared?"

Caught up in the afternoon commotion, Beth had completely forgotten about the gowns that needed mending.

"Yes, my lady," she lied.

Eleanore's eyes narrowed. "Good. Bring them to my chamber."

4

BETH

Beth sat perched on the small stool in her chamber, squinting to thread a needle with trembling hands beneath the fading light from the small window. Lady Eleanore's gown was draped over her lap in ample folds. After Beth had explained her predicament, Annie—still in her blissful state—released her for the rest of the afternoon. As Beth had hurried off, she heard Annie order Kat to finish Beth's tasks, and she felt her stomach tighten with unease at the retribution the girl might conjure in the days to come.

Beth rushed through the first gown, cursing her clumsy hands. But, eventually, remembering Lady Sarah's encouragement, her stitching grew steadier and more precise. Each stitch had to be perfect. Surely, no second chances would be given.

Making the neckline smaller was straightforward, and she was grateful for the simplicity. The second dress was more complicated. She had been told to bring up the sleeve length two inches but had neglected to measure Lady Eleanore's arm length, and she prayed the alteration would not be too little or too much.

After a while, both gowns were complete, but the hour was late. Beth swiftly folded the yards of delicate fabric into a neat stack. She'd have to hurry to deliver the gowns and pray Eleanore was a forgiving mistress.

Beth's arms ached under the heavy weight, but as she rushed to Lady Eleanore's den, Kat met her in the servant's hall. The girl had finally finished her day's work, along with Beth's chores too.

Kat thrust out her blistered palms, and Beth winced at the raw skin. "This is what I get for scrubbing the worktables with salt and vinegar!" she spat.

Beth took a deep breath and steadied herself against Kat's rage. "There is a tallow paste I can make to heal them," she said evenly.

Kat bent her face close to Beth's. "I don't want your silly remedy!" she secthed. "I want you to remember your place!"

Beth shook her head, mindful of the precious time slipping away. "If you don't want my help move aside," she said, pushing past Kat.

"Watch yourself!" Kat called after her. "You think yourself my better . . . and I will prove you wrong!"

Kat's voice faded in Beth's wake as she hurried along, fearing the admonishing that awaited her from Lady Eleanore.

As she strode past the library, she glanced inside the open door. The heavy tables and armchairs were gone. Instead, a makeshift worktable and a tall wooden scaffold sat in the center of the room.

"Beg your pardon, miss," a voice said from behind.

Startled, she moved from the threshold as a young man with rounded shoulders struggled with a large trunk. He was thin and wore a laborer's woolen doublet with a leather cap that covered most of his light-colored hair. His face was amiable, and his eyes were expressive and deep-set.

The man stumbled into the library, dropping the trunk near the worktable with a loud thud.

"They're heavier than they appear," he said sheepishly. "My name is John." He tipped his cap to her. "I'm Master Owen's apprentice."

"I'm Beth," she replied shyly.

John peered at her armful of fabric and sewing basket. "You are a seamstress for the manor?" he asked curiously.

She blushed. "Of sorts," she answered. "I was told you're making repairs to the library."

"My master, Nicholas, is performing renovations," John said. "He's a gifted carpenter, and I've much to learn from him."

Beth admired the earnestness in his voice and the respect he held for his master. She felt a kindred spirit with the man since, like her, he was new to the manor.

"Where are you from?" she asked.

John's face clouded as if he were unsure of how to answer. Then he quickly said, "Northumberland."

"I've never been," Beth said, eager for him to share more.

John looked at her sagging arms, still full. "I can help you carry those, if you like."

Suddenly, Beth's stomach lurched in a panic as she remembered Lady Eleanore's orders. Again, she had forgotten the task at hand.

She dipped a quick curtsy. "I must go . . . I'm terribly sorry," she said in a rush.

Beth hurried to her mistress's chamber and tapped lightly on the door, entering on Lady Eleanore's command.

Her ladyship sat at her writing desk, quill in hand. "You're late. I expected you'd be more dutiful," she said, not looking up from the note she was writing. Her tone was not of anger but disappointment.

"My sincere apologies, my lady," Beth said, afraid to lift her eyes. Her nerves fluttered like a moth trapped under a glass.

"What kept you?"

Beth's throat tightened. "I wanted to make the alterations perfect, my lady. My hope was to please your ladyship . . . make you proud to wear whichever gown you chose. It took longer than expected . . ." she stammered, ashamed to have failed at her first important task. Tears filled her eyes. "Perhaps I am not the servant you hoped for. If you wish, I'll gather my belongings and leave the manor immediately."

"Leave the gowns on the settee," Lady Eleanore said, not inquiring further about Beth's tardiness or answering the question. Instead, she placed the quill into the inkwell and carefully folded the paper then sealed it with wax. "Deliver this note to Master Owen. You'll find him in the guest quarters. You needn't wait for a reply."

"Yes, my lady," Beth said shakily, taking the note with a trembling hand. Her mind swam with bewilderment. The reprimand was no rebuke at all.

Lady Eleanore looked at her pointedly. "No one needs to know what passes between me and our guests. Understand? I trust in your utmost discretion in these matters. Go now."

"Of course, my lady."

When Beth arrived at the carpenter's apartments, a man small in stature greeted her. His graying hair was short and thinning on top. Silver spectacles sat perched on the end of his wide nose. His eyes were kind, and his voice was amiable but timid as he welcomed Beth inside, closing the door behind her.

The man introduced himself as Nicholas Owen and instructed her to call him by his given name. The room was spacious and comfortable, with a desk, oversized uphol-stered chairs, and a table. Two beds sat on opposite sides of the fireplace.

"From Lady Eleanore," Beth said and handed him the note with a curtsy.

Nicholas did not open the sealed paper but set it on the desk. His left leg awkwardly curled inward as he walked, hobbling his gait, and Beth thought the burden must make his trade as a carpenter difficult.

"You're Beth," he said. "Lady Eleanore spoke of you. She said you'll see to our needs and assist with errands."

"I am at your service, sir," Beth replied earnestly.

Before he could reply, the door swung open, and Gareth and John entered, each man carrying a trunk with Fritz wagging his tail behind them.

"I'm sorry, sir," Gareth said to Nicholas, shaking his head at Fritz, who was busy sniffing the man's leather boots.

Nicholas pulled his spectacles down to get a better look. "Is this your dog?"

Gareth shrugged. "Not mine, really," he answered with a sheepish grin. "But he thinks he is, and I don't mind."

"Well, you're fortunate. God's creatures are heaven's gift to humanity, and your little dog is always welcome here," Nicholas said, patting Fritz's head.

Beth raised an eyebrow and grinned. "But not in Annie's kitchen . . ."

Gareth returned her jest with a wry smile.

John removed his cap and wiped his brow. "This is the last of them," he said to Nicholas, pointing to the trunks.

"Good. Put them over there," Nicholas instructed, gesturing to an empty corner. "I'm eager to start tomorrow. There is much to do."

Beth and Gareth left the men to unpack and headed down the hall to their respective duties.

They walked in silence. The thought of journeying with Gareth to Surrey, knowing he wished to go alone, annoyed Beth. She never intended to experience the village as an unwanted traveling companion.

Unable to stand the silence, she finally said, "Master Owen and his apprentice seem quite amiable."

Gareth nodded. "If Nicholas allows it, I thought I'd take John to Surrey. Show him the village."

Anger rose in Beth's gut. Of course, Gareth would welcome male company over her own. She pictured both men bellying up with a tankard at some alehouse or squandering their coin at a dicing-house.

She squelched her irritation and said, "I'm sure he'd appreciate that. He told me he was from Northumberland. It must be hard being so far away from home."

Gareth stopped short. His brow furrowed in confusion. "Northumberland? John told me he was from Derby."

Beth returned his gaze, equally puzzled. "Perhaps he misspoke," she said, unable to provide a better explanation.

"Maybe," Gareth replied and hurried back to the stables.

5

BETH

Bodsworth Chapel was sparse, with soaring, clear glass windows, a few dozen pews, and a polished wood pulpit. Beth took account of the household in attendance at Sunday service. It was strange to see the pew reserved for Lord and Lady Sheffield empty. She peered behind her at the array of manor servants and noticed Gareth's absence as well.

Beth's mind did not drift as usual during the long, drawn-out sermon, for the prospect of seeing the village, despite Gareth's taking exception to her company, kept her alert and attentive. Grateful to escape Kat's watchful eyes, Beth slipped away as the congregants filed out the door.

Free and unnoticed, Beth saw Gareth waiting by the stonewall farthest away from the chapel and churchgoers. A massive horse, no less than sixteen hands and black as a moonless night, stood beside him, a packsaddle straddling his wide back. Warm air puffed from its nostrils as the animal shook its silken mane and flicked its tail, keeping the biting flies at bay.

Beth approached, and Gareth greeted her with a cool nod.

Ignoring the slight, Beth set the woven basket down and stroked the horse's muscled neck.

"He's beautiful," she said as the gelding bobbed his head at her touch.

"His name is Blackthorne. I've cared for him since he was a foal." Gareth gave the horse an affectionate pat and untied a water jug from the packsaddle and handed it to her. "Here. Drink. I'll get more along the way."

Beth took a large swallow and handed him back the jug.

The autumn sun spread across the surrounding hills in a palette of golden fields and russet hills, warming the brisk, clean air which filled Beth's lungs as she inhaled deeply, grateful to be away from the smoke of the kitchen fires. The silence was welcome, too. Idle conversation would only foster a false camaraderie, meant only to fill the space between them. Yet, the silence was short-lived.

"Have you family back at Abury?" Gareth asked, kicking a stone as they walked.

"I'm an orphan."

Gareth paused, then said, "No brothers? No sisters?"

"None."

"Sorry for that."

Beth shrugged. "Don't be. It's hard to miss something you've never known." The lie left her mouth with practiced ease, and she continued. "My family worked at Abury as far back as my grandparents. That much I know. They died of fever when I was quite young. I don't remember them at all. Lady Barrell and the undercook raised me with great care, and I am forever grateful."

Gareth let out a long whistle. "Ah, the fever. It nearly took half the village a few years back."

Quietness again settled between them, and Beth swallowed hard as she stared down at the brownish grass growing between the carriage ruts. Recounting her past always brought up a bygone of drifting specters, a resurrection of shadows without form or feature.

Gareth's tone brightened. "I'm the oldest of the Montgomerys. I have a younger brother, Rafe. Someday I'll leave Bodsworth and strike out on my own. Become a tenant farmer. Maybe travel abroad and make my fortune. I believe my destiny to be my own, you see." His boot struck another stone, sending it down the road farther than the first. "Once my brother is old enough, he'll take my place at the manor—if Father allows it . . ." His face darkened as he looked away.

Beth had never considered venturing out alone. The thought was peculiar. Could such freedom ever be possible? Gareth was secure within a family, one that needed him, yet it did not satisfy him. Instead, it hemmed him in like a funeral shroud. If he understood the pain of not having a family, perhaps he would not be so quick to get away from his own.

As they made their way, Beth's upturned face basked in the sun's warmth. The late autumn frost slipped off leaves and blades of grass like a dressing gown. Winter's blast was sure to follow and promised a treacherous mix of ice, mud, and snow, making journeys to the village less frequent and fraught with danger.

After a while, the gurgle of a quick-moving river overtook the monotony of Blackthorne's clopping hooves. Beth watched as Gareth assessed the swift current. He pulled back on the harness, and Blackthorne's gait slowed to a halt.

"Good time to refill," he said, untying the water jug and nodding at the river. He led Blackthorne off the road to a patch of brown grass where a few stubborn tender blades still poked through. "Stay here." He thrust the harness rope at Beth and trampled down the riverbank, thick with brush.

Blackthorne shifted beside her, tail swishing lazily. Hand on her hip, Beth watched as Gareth scrambled along the whooshing gray water, his skillful steps quick and light. Finally, he stooped and refilled the jug, but instead of coming back, he set the clay pot between two stones and walked farther down the river.

"Where are you going?" Beth called to him, irritated he had ventured so far away, but she received no answer as he disappeared around the bend.

Anger surged through her. It was unsafe to leave her alone and unaccompanied on the open road. With the painful memory of Peter's slap, she pulled Blackthorne to a small tree and wrapped the rope around a low branch. She may have been a lowly servant, but she wasn't Gareth's, and she refused to be ordered about, especially if following those orders left her vulnerable.

Mindful of the thorn bushes, Beth made her way down the bank, following Gareth's path. With determined steps, she strode past the water jug and around the river's bend. There she found Gareth, boots in the shallows, with a wooden spool and a fishing line, casting into the dark, gray water. Death was the punishment for poaching. All fish in the waterways belonged to the manor house, and the punishment for thievery was as swift as it was certain.

Beth watched as Gareth tugged the line and twirled the spool, pulling a squirming trout from the water. He was reckless. Rude. Full of himself. But as he gently removed the hook and placed the fish in his satchel, his tenderness gave her pause. She watched as he cast the line again. Clearly, the risky endeavor was not new to him. In no time, he had hauled up another fat trout. It was clear now why Gareth was not keen on her company. A potential witness to his crime only brought more danger.

Satisfied, he rolled up the line and turned to leave, catching Beth's angry stare. He sauntered over with a brazen grin. "Not to worry. Lord Charles won't miss two fish," he said, giving the bag a gentle pat.

"His lordship will have you swinging from the highest limb if I tell the warden," she answered, just as boldly.

Gareth stood and brushed his hands on his breeches. "You won't tell," he replied smoothly, scrambling back up to the road.

Beth grabbed the water jug and followed him. "Won't I?"

Gareth turned and leveled his eyes at her. "You didn't stop me. You didn't yell for help. You did nothing. I'll say you were in on it. I've given it plenty of thought." Gareth took the jug from her and secured it to the saddle.

"You're a thief and a liar," she snapped.

"Call me what you will," Gareth said, untying Blackthorne and leading him back to the road. "But we all do what we must."

Beth's temper eased to a simmer as they made their way in silence, passing harvested orchards and duck-filled ponds, cows grazing in meadows, and wheat fields cut to the quick; the wheat berries already hulled and ground into coarse flour for the winter months ahead.

Soon, they came upon a small farmhouse with a thatched roof, a cowshed, and several outbuildings. Neatly stacked stone walls lined the surrounding fields, freshly harrowed. Without warning, Gareth stopped at the cobbled path leading to the farmhouse door. He eyed the road up and back, then let out a long whistle between his thumb and forefinger. A moment later, the wooden door creaked open and a slight woman with graying hair appeared in the doorway. Gareth was already hurrying down the path toward her.

Dressed in a simple frock and apron, she took Gareth's shoulders and assessed him up and down, then folded him in her arms in a tight embrace. Beth watched the reunion with a pang of longing. A memory stirred of warm bread and acceptance but was gone as quickly as it'd come.

They shared a few words before Gareth handed her a trout from his bag, and with a quick peck on his cheek, the woman took the fish and closed the door.

"Your mother?" Beth asked when he returned.

Gareth nodded and adjusted Blackthorne's harness. "My family struggles despite my position at the manor house. Times are hard. Winter will only make it harder. I help when I can."

Beth pondered his words and the sagging thatch on the cowshed roof. "Why not give your mother both fish, then?"

Gareth's jaw tightened as he led Blackthorne on without an answer.

Eventually, the countryside boasted larger farms, outposts, and tanneries, and before long, the winding cart road turned into a proper street, swarming with people as they entered the village.

They walked amid the routine of peasant life, a swirl of bustling commotion. Women hurried on their way with tasks and errands to complete. Some bore baskets brimming with produce, while others maneuvered carts laden with nuts and berries gathered from the forests. Horses dragged hay wagons down mud-thick streets as children darted in and out of the chaos with playful abandon. Conversations mingled together over the calls of vendors hawking their wares.

"Edward Hasting's wife birthed another babe last night. That makes ten now, I think," Beth heard a woman say.

"At this rate, who can keep count?" another woman said, and they both exchanged rueful glances.

The stench of horses, mules, and sheep blended with the aroma of baking bread. The pungent scent of wood smoke puffed from stone chimneys. Along the way, they collected the items on the list, including string, a marking gauge, an awl, yards of white cloth, and olive oil. As Beth added the items to the hamper, she thought it strange that carpenters would need cloth and oil to repair a library.

"What's left?" Gareth asked as Beth slipped the list back inside her apron.

"Nails," she said, "two buckets' worth. We'll need to find a blacksmith."

Gareth stiffened. "I know where to find nails," he snapped, his face set in a rigid scowl.

Beth flinched at the edge in his voice, unsure what had triggered the gruff response.

A few blocks down, they came upon a blacksmith shop. Outside was a worn sign with a crude carving of a horseshoe and mallet. A few horses tethered to the hitching post near the entrance whinnied and snorted for attention. The double doors to the shed were open, and Gareth and Beth stepped inside.

"Good morning, Father," Gareth called out over the clanging of metal.

Beth's eyes widened.

George Montgomery stood at the enormous bellows. Both hands gripped the long wooden handle as he pumped the air in and out like a tremendous lung. The coals glowed dull black to fiery red as the air breathed new life into the hard lumps.

Gareth's father was a broad, formidable man. His muscular arms pulled the handle with ease. He wore a sleeveless shirt, long breeches, and a heavy leather apron. A thick cap protected his head from wayward sparks.

"Good morning," Gareth shouted again at his father to no avail.

In the corner sat a young boy, no older than ten years, sorting a crate of finished hand tools. "Gareth!" he yelled cheerfully.

"My brother, Rafe," he told Beth as the boy left his post and ran to them, his face glowing with delight.

Beth smiled, a wistful ache blooming inside her as the boy bounded toward his brother.

Gareth playfully tousled the lad's sand-colored locks. "Father, has you working harder than a pack mule, I see."

"I don't mind," Rafe answered, eyeing Beth with interest. "It beats mucking the cowshed for Mother."

The whooshing bellows stopped as Gareth's father approached.

"This is Beth, her ladyship's maidservant," Gareth told his father before he could ask. "We've been sent for supplies."

"We need nails, sir, if you please," Beth stammered awkwardly.

George grunted, then turned his gaze to Gareth. "Master Telford stopped in yesterday for new horse bits. Mentioned you've been much preoccupied with things other than your stable duties." Soot darkened his cheeks, and his penetrating eyes expressed much disapproval. "He speaks of a girl who visits the stables frequently." His dark eyes flicked back to Beth.

"It is the maidservant, Kat, from the kitchen, Father, and I don't encourage her."

Beth stiffened. Perhaps Kat's designs on Gareth were more advanced than she'd thought.

George grunted again. "Yet she still comes," he growled. "She is an unwelcome distraction. Make yourself indispensable. It is the only way to rise in the ranks."

Gareth pulled back his shoulders. "I don't intend to rise in the ranks, Father," he answered, a sharp edge in his voice. "I wish to make my way in this world. I've told you that many times!"

Beth swallowed hard as the two men locked eyes, both stubborn and unyielding. Gareth's carefree spirit and sense of adventure clashed with his father's grounded, practical nature. Between them stood a gulf.

A hollowness settled over Beth. She had no memory of such arguments. No father's voice rising in anger. No guiding hand to offer advice—nothing at all.

The opening door and the arrival of two men interrupted the battle of wills. Beth's blood ran cold. The cleric and the lord who'd struck Peter stood before her. Their eyes surveyed the humble shop as if it were an insult.

"No one has shod them!" the lord shouted at George, motioning to the horses outside.

"There is work ahead of you, sir," George said, his tone switching from that of an angry father to a diplomatic tradesman. He gestured to the pitchfork in the forge.

The old cleric stepped forward. "My name is Reverend William Holbrook and this," he nodded at the scowl-faced man, "is Sir Richard Bayne. Her Majesty commissions us to enforce the penal rule of Protestants." He peered at young Rafe, who half hid behind his brother. "The boy did not mention the urgency of the matter when the squire delivered our horses?"

"The boy did not," George answered, his face flushing.

The scowling man, Richard Bayne, suddenly lunged at Rafe, brandishing the boy by the neck scruff. Rafe let out a yelp as Bayne flung him to the dirt floor. He raised a gloved hand to punish Rafe further, but Gareth grabbed Bayne from behind and threw him onto the trestle table. Nails and farming tools scattered across the ground.

Bayne sprang from the floor; his eyes crazed with shock and rage. He unsheathed his sword and pointed it at Gareth. "Boy thinks he's a hero!"

Beth wanted to scream for the fighting to stop, but as with when the man had slapped Peter, she found herself rooted in place, her battering heart the only part of her that moved.

George grabbed the firepit poker and took two daunting steps toward Bayne.

"Cease at once!" the cleric shouted. Everyone halted as if the very words held the queen's power. "Have our horses ready by day's end," he told George, then turned to Sir Bayne. "Come. We've no time for folly when graver sins await judgment." His tone was that of a master bringing a dog to heel. "We must hurry to the priest discovered at the Hastings house. Have the men bring fresh horses."

They turned to leave, but the reverend suddenly stopped. His cold, granite eyes settled on Beth. Her heart raced as he gave her a long, curious look. "You are the girl from the road. The one with the careless driver."

Beth nodded, her words lost to her once again.

"Did you find your way to . . ." he paused, "Bodsworth Hall, was it?" His voice was calm, disarmingly so, as if the current situation was beneath him.

"Yes, my lord," she answered softly.

He turned to Bayne with a humorless smile. "Come," he said, and the two men departed.

George wasted no time in assessing Rafe. "Are you hurt, son?" He held the boy by the shoulders and studied his face.

"No, Father."

Satisfied, George's voice took on a more admonishing tenor. "Why did you not tell me about the horses?"

Gareth stepped forward and wrapped a protective arm around his brother. "He made a mistake, Father. That is all. I am sure he's sorry. Am I right, Rafe?"

Rafe rubbed his tear-stained face as his head bobbed up and down, his eyes bright with fresh tears. "I am very sorry, Father."

George's chest swelled like a bellow, and he sighed, patting Rafe's tiny head. His eyes narrowed at Gareth and Beth. "If I am to get those horses shod today, I'll need help."

As Beth lugged water from a nearby stream, she was doubly glad to have chosen her work shoes that morning for the walk and not her Sunday latchet slippers. Gareth and George worked at a punishing rhythm, hammering out the horseshoes, while Rafe fetched a meal from his mother, happy to be free of work for a while.

"I feel for Edward Hastings," Beth heard George tell Gareth as she emptied the bucket into the water barrel. "The priest's fate is sealed. He'll go to the tower and die horribly. Edward will most likely pay a heavy fine, maybe worse, and with all those children and a new babe, I don't know how they'll manage."

Gareth turned to Beth. "The cleric said he remembered you from the road."

She set the empty bucket down and sat on a stool to rest. "Yes. They stopped me and my driver, Peter, on the road to Bodsworth."

"They stop everyone," George added sourly. "No one is without suspicion."

Beth was about to speak of the violence Peter had endured, but little Rafe burst through the door, breathless. A woven basket hung from one arm, and a loaf of bread was tucked under the other. His face was pale, and his eyes were round with fright.

"Rafe? What is it, son?" George said.

"They've brought Master Hastings to the scaffold! They mean to flog him! The old man with the pointed hat demands everyone in the village bear witness!"

George paused for a moment and then slipped off his gloves. "Damn them! May God give Edward the strength to bear it." He shook his head. "We cannot ignore the cleric's ruling."

Beth looked pleadingly at Gareth. Witnessing such inhumanity was more than she could bear.

"All must attend. It is demanded," Gareth said to her before she could say the words. "The queen's men will take account of those who don't obey."

George closed and bolted the smithy doors, and they joined the throng of villagers surging toward the crossroads, the heart of village life. Gareth's mother appeared, long-faced and tearful, and took her place beside her husband.

"Father made me come!" Rafe wailed, burying his little face in her apron.

She wrapped her arms around the boy and gave George a wary look. "Can't I take him away from here?"

George's eyes swept the crowd, and he shook his head. "No, Agnes, you know they'll take notice of who's missing."

The crowd's restlessness grew. Beth watched in terror as soldiers dragged Edward Hastings from his hovel near the village center. She glanced down the road at the pitiful structure—its roof gaping with a hole that sufficed as a vent for the cooking smoke. The walls, crudely packed with mud and stick, could have belonged to a livestock shed. She could scarcely imagine how twelve souls dwelt in such misery.

Edward was a mere husk of a man—shoulders rounded, arms scarcely thicker than tinder sticks. Blood dripped around his mouth from the beating already delivered by the soldiers. His dazed wife stumbled behind him, still in her stained birthing smock, with a trail of crying children behind her. A tiny bundle wrapped in cloth wailed in the crook of her arm.

A man leaned closer to George. His sour breath stank of ale.

"They found the priest an hour ago giving the babe a baptism," he said in a low voice.

"Twas not a problem last week. Only saying the Mass was forbidden," George replied.

The man's rumy eyes widened. "Everything Catholic is illegal now, my friend. Her Majesty decreed it two days ago after the trouble with the rebels up north." He lowered his voice even further. "You'd think she would've given more time for news to spread and the law to take hold before making it treason."

"Just as well," Beth heard the woman next to them say, "the queen's right to punish the clergy who keep the

Mass in Latin and not allow decent folk to read the Bible in English. I heard the saintly relics taken from the abbey were only pig bones and lamb's blood! Flogging is too good for him. That's what I say!" She peered at George, Gareth, Beth, and little Thomas. "You aren't Catholic now, are ya?" Her eyes studied their faces closely.

"I am not," George shot back, planting his hands on his hips. "But what if I were? Is that what we do now? Turn on friends and neighbors?"

Beth looked at Agnes. Her face went pale as her husband trod on dangerous ground. Her eyes silently begged him to stop. Yet, he continued.

"I follow rules. Those who frequent my smithy know I'm a fair man. I abide by the Church of England, and for a year now we have lived in harmony, side by side, Catholics and Protestants alike. Her Majesty tallied loyal subjects over religion." His voice grew louder as the surrounding onlookers listened in.

"I'd wager most of Surrey wakes on the morn and goes about their business thinking only of the day's work. They pay no mind to how their neighbors worship or who they pray to when a child falls ill, a horse goes lame, or the village well runs dry."

"Aye, aye . . ." murmured a few voices nearby.

Despair and anger rose in George's voice. "They care only that their children are well, horses mend, and water is abundant, and whatever God answers that plea is the one for them."

"What about the abbey that paid the manor tax on the backs of villagers and the travelers on pilgrimage fooled into buying useless relics?" a voice from the crowd challenged.

Before George could answer, two men pulled a wagon bearing a metal cage to the front of the crowd. Inside, an old priest with a puckered face rocked back and forth on his knees, murmuring prayers for a deliverance that never came. Soldiers dragged Edward up the scaffold stairs, tore off his ragged shirt, and bound his wrists to the whipping post.

Beth's legs wavered beneath her, and she clutched her skirts, steadying herself.

Reverend Holbrook climbed to the top of the scaffold with measured steps and strode forth to the center of the platform. His black, ankle-length cassock brushed the rough planks as he clutched a leather-bound Bible to his chest. His pinched face turned to speak as the bound, bare-backed Edward whimpered behind him.

"Dutiful people of Surrey," he began, his voice lilting and bright, as if addressing a wedding feast. "I bring to you a wretched soul in direct disobedience of Her Majesty's penal decree of religious obedience." He turned his gaze to Edward. "This man was found harboring a papist priest—one caught performing a secret baptism on this innocent babe." His claw-like hand rose, a knobby finger singling out Mistress Hastings and the trembling family cowering before the crowd. "In times past, our most gracious queen showed mercy toward such heresy and treachery—but no more. Since Pope Pius, in his arrogance, has issued his Papal Bull of excommunication against our sovereign, Her Majesty shall henceforth show no leniency. From this day forward, all who refuse to acknowledge her as the Supreme Head of the Church of England, and persist in the idolatry of Rome, shall be deemed traitors."

Holbrook stepped aside as Bayne reached the top of the platform, brandishing a whip made of long leather straps embellished with bits of metal.

"God be with him," Beth whispered, dread coiling in her chest, as she swayed against Gareth. His hand slipped into hers, and she let it rest there, grateful for the comfort.

With the slightest of nods from the reverend, Bayne raised the weapon of torture high above his head and brought it down hard across Hastings's back.

George shielded Rafe's peeking eyes as Edward's scream pierced the air like an arrow sprung from a crossbow. He twisted and bucked but could not escape the whip. Blood sprayed across the straw.

The bitter taste of bile rose in Beth's throat as Edward's skin flayed open before her with each brutal strike. Again and again, the whip fell as Mistress Hastings wailed.

Finally, her husband's screams grew silent as he went limp. Yet, Bayne continued the punishment with crazed eyes and a sweaty brow until the reverend lightly touched his shoulder to stop him, but not before he landed one last strike.

In the deafening silence, the crowd dispersed as a few villagers cut poor Edward down and carried him off. Some good-hearted women tended to Mistress Hastings, leading her away along with her crying children. Soldiers pulled the wagon carrying the priest behind Reverend Holbrook and Bayne as they moved along with the rest of the queen's retinue. The job was done. A harsh warning had been delivered. A message delivered in blood.

6

GARETH

A lively fire blazed in the fireplace, casting a warm glow over Lady Eleanore's den. But the warmth did little to ease the chill that hung in the room. Lord Charles and his wife sat on matching velvet armchairs facing Gareth and Beth, perched on a settee. The day's events were still a painful blight, and Gareth glanced at Beth, who sipped the wine their lordships had insisted they drink as if in a trance.

Word of Edward Hastings's flogging had spread to Bodsworth Hall long before Gareth's and Beth's arrival. Grief, suspicion, and dread settled over the manor like a fog.

Except for clipped orders in the stable, Lord Charles had been little more than a shadow to Gareth. With his detailed instructions and devotion to his horses, Lord Charles demanded much from Master Telford and the stable attendants. Many times, Gareth had swallowed his contempt for the man, as his prized stallions lived in greater comfort than most of the villagers who struggled to pay the manor taxes. Now, as he and Beth drank wine beside each other like two obedient hounds, the bitterness curdled in his gut.

Gareth stared into the silver cup. The horrible afternoon seared forever in his mind, and his thoughts swirled like the dark wine.

Charles finally spoke after an uncomfortable silence. "There is much to discuss," he said, glancing at his wife. "We'd best get on with it."

"Agreed," said Eleanore softly.

Charles stood and paced before them, reminding Gareth of one of his many spirited geldings. "As you know, Master Owen and his apprentice are repairing the library." He paused as if unsure of himself. "What you need to know is why. After bearing witness to today's horrible account, it's time for the truth."

Eleanore shot him a wary look, but he pressed on. "Master Owen is not only renovating—he is creating. Building something of great importance. Constructing a space to hide the hunted from the hunters."

"A priest hole," Eleanore cut in, unable to contain herself. "To protect those who administer the sacraments and hear the confession of sinners."

"You're Catholic?" Beth blurted out.

Charles pressed his finger to his lips. "Not so loud. Yes—we are Catholic. And in these times, that is a dangerous secret to keep. What you saw today was a mere glimpse of the peril we face—what all of us who keep the old faith endure. Providing a haven for priests to tend their flock and perform the sacraments is critical. The priest hunters are merciless and will be relentless now that they have reason to continue their pursuit in Surrey."

The flush from the wine drained from Gareth's face. The secret they revealed meant torture or worse. He glanced at Beth, whose face was ashen with worry.

"We cannot trust many," Eleanore said, her eyes pleading with them. "Help is needed. We must complete the priest hole quickly to protect those we shelter."

Gareth looked up from his cup. "Why us?"

Charles's pacing halted mid-stride as his angry eyes pierced Gareth like daggers. "You steal fish from my river. You sell them on the sly to travelers and those who pilgrimage." His gaze turned icy. "Thought you'd get away with it, did you?"

Gareth's mouth fell open. The urge to flee gripped him. He spied the door that opened onto the hall leading to the servant staircase. It was close but not close enough. The lord was still young enough to give a good chase. He looked back down into the cup.

"You need money. That much is clear. But not just for your family." Charles stroked his beard. "There must be another reason. Tell me, why do you steal my fish?"

Gareth saw from Beth's horrified eyes that she also understood that his fate was sealed. He clenched his jaw and glared at Charles, rage flaring in his chest.

How dare Lord Charles, or any man, lay claim to all the fish in God's rivers. Was it not the Almighty who set them swimming there? To confess his reason for poaching meant laying bare his heart for all to see. His anger ebbed, leaving confusion in its wake. Perhaps it was time.

"I meant to leave the manor someday, my lord," he said at last, his voice sorrowful, yet steady, "once my brother was old enough to take my place. I would've made my own way in the world, perhaps as a tenant farmer in my own right. Lived on my own terms, not shine saddles or haul barrels till my dying day." Gareth lowered his head. The dream was over and so, he feared, was his life.

"I see," said Charles, nodding slowly. "But you need not steal from me. You aim high, and I commend your adventurous spirit, but don't devalue your dream with ill-gotten coins. I will pay you, fairly and well, if you help Master Owen complete the priest hole—and keep it a secret."

Gareth blinked, surprised by the generous offer. Perhaps he was mistaken about Lord Charles. Then again, the man was desperate and in dire need of help. Without the priest hole, Gareth was quite certain he'd be swinging from the gallows that very day. Aiding the Sheffields was, in truth, no request—it was a requirement. Either way, he was cornered. But cornered and alive was better than hanged. There was no choice but to agree.

"Thank you, my lord. I am at your service, and your plan is safe with me," he said, bowing his head, the bitter taste of defeat on his tongue.

Charles returned to his seat next to Eleanore as she rose to address Beth.

Lady Eleanor's level gaze at the girl made Gareth wonder what news was to befall her.

"I haven't been entirely truthful with you, Beth," her ladyship began, arms folded tightly.

Gareth prayed that whatever truth Eleanore meant to reveal would not break the girl beside him, who was already as fragile as a finch after the horrors in the village.

"I knew Lady Barrell. More than I let on," she said, voice trembling. "Sarah was my aunt—my mother's sister. Our families were . . . estranged."

Beth's brow furrowed. "Why? Why were they estranged?" Her voice was tight as she absentmindedly folded and unfolded the crease in her apron.

Gareth turned to Lord Charles. "Perhaps this is enough for one day."

But Eleanore pressed on. "I was a child—barely five years of age—but the terror haunts me still. It was Christmastide . . . late and snowing. My mother rushed into the nursery here at Bodsworth, rousing my brothers, sisters, and me. She told of Queen Mary's inquisitors scouring the village for Protestants."

Beth's head tilted. "But you're Catholic."

Eleanore's eyes widened, recalling a past that still haunted her. "No. We weren't. Not then. My father served King Henry, who severed ties with the Vatican." She moved to the fireplace, the flames silhouetting the soft features of her profile.

"Henry, the arrogant fool, declared himself head of the Church of England," Charles cut in. "Renounced the Catholic Church. Seized its assets. When Mary took the throne, the country had veered back to Catholicism. With it came persecution."

"What does that have to do with Lady Sarah?" Beth asked, her narrowed eyes unflinching.

"My aunt refused us shelter," Eleanore whispered, the memory playing out amidst the burning logs. "We'd fled to Abury, desperate, with the inquisitors at our heels. My mother begged her sister—your Lady Sarah—to let us in. But she turned us away. All of us."

Beth's brow was glossy with sweat. "I don't believe you!" she said, anger rising in her voice.

"Oh, but she did, Beth—my mother, father, and six children all turned away at her gate."

Beth shook her head in disbelief. "But why? Why do such a thing?"

"Perhaps she was weak-minded from that tyrant husband, Lord Thomas. It was common knowledge the man sought favor with Queen Mary, hoping for a seat on her privy council," Eleanore scoffed. "Denouncing Protestantism meant nothing to him. He became a Catholic as easily as changing undergarments. Forced Sarah to do the same. And . . ." she breathed deeply and turned to Beth. "He gave evidence against Protestants to prove his loyalty."

"Where did you go?" Beth stared at Lady Eleanore trance-like, her eyes glistening.

"To Devonshire, at first. A trusted cousin took us in until the day when even that was no longer safe. The inquisitors were quite adept at rooting out their enemies, even perceived ones. Eventually, we embraced Catholicism—to survive."

Beth's eyes widened. "Then return to the Church of England! Convert again and be done with it! Live in peace," she snapped, as if the answer was simple.

Eleanore turned back to the fire. "Until it happens again? And again?" She placed her hand on the stone mantel. "Peace bought with cowardice is no peace at all. Charles and I have found solace in Queen Mary's religion. We embrace it as our own and pray for the souls Queen Mary wronged. She was reckless and misguided, haunted by the mistreatment of her mother. We pray for your grandparent's souls, too . . ."

Beth stood abruptly, spilling wine on the Persian carpet. The red stain spread and seeped into the delicate fibers like blood. Gareth rose as well, reaching for her arm, unsure of her intent.

"My family died of fever! All of them!" Beth cried, her voice cracking.

Gareth tightened his grip on Beth's arm as she struggled to pull away.

Eleanore's face collapsed with sorrow. "Your parents died of fever. That much is true. But your grandparents perished at the hands of Lord and Lady Barrell, who gave them over to the inquisitors. They were martyred. Burned at the stake."

Gareth caught Beth as she sank to the floor, cradling her head in his lap. Her eyes fluttered closed. Wisps of damp strands spread across her wet forehead. He peered up at the stricken Charles and Eleanore.

"Take her to the maid's quarters across from my bed-chamber," Eleanore told Gareth. "Deliver her belongings there, too. Have my chambermaid make her comfortable."

The following morning, the news of Edward Hastings's death reached the manor with little surprise. The apothecaries and nursemaids were unable to stem the bleeding from his countless wounds. Many whispered of God's mercy in spiriting away the tortured man, sparing him a long and drawn-out demise. Others wondered how his wife and children would survive the fast-approaching winter.

In the courtyard, Gareth wiped the sweat from his brow after countless trips delivering wood to the library. Nicholas's project was twofold—create enough construction havoc to conceal the building of the priest hole, and to replace sections of the perfectly sound library floor as a diversion. Gareth had decided early on that until the work was finished, he was better off keeping to himself.

His thoughts were interrupted when Kat crossed the muddy yard, a hamper swinging from her hand. Hastily, he turned and busied himself, loading the wheelbarrow with the planks Nicholas requested, but it was too late.

"Beth's satchel and trunk are missing. She didn't sleep in our bedchamber last night. Where is the wench?" Kat stood like a statue, a hand planted firmly on her hip.

Gareth reached for another plank and placed it in the barrow. "She fainted. Lady Eleanore believes she's in shock from the flogging and is looking after her," he said. "The mistress wants Beth to serve Master Owen on tasks and errands, so I think she plans to keep her for a while."

"Why not me? I've been here longer and have never given the mistress any trouble." Her eyes bore into him.

Gareth wanted to remind Kat of all the mischief she had caused long before Beth had arrived with her idle gossip and bickering ways, but he shrugged and answered, "How am I to know such things?"

"I've seen how the mistress looks at Beth," Kat murmured. "Strange, isn't it? How some folk land on their feet, no matter what the trouble? Abury Manor goes to pieces, and poor little Beth ends up at Bodsworth. . . as her ladyship's favorite, no less."

Gareth scuffed his boot heel against the packed dirt and bit down on his lower lip.

Kat looked at her basket, and her mood brightened. "I'm bringing this food hamper to the Hastings as a show of goodwill from the Sheffields. I'll ask Annie if you can escort me, if you like."

"Don't," Gareth said, shaking his head. "There is too much to be done, and I've wasted time already carrying on with you. I must go." He lifted the wheelbarrow and pushed it along. Kat scowled in his wake before scurrying away in a huff.

When Gareth arrived, the library was a flurry of cutting and hammering. Nicholas's graying hair was covered in fine sawdust as he pushed and pulled the teeth of the saw through one of the remaining planks. A row of sawhorses waited for Gareth's delivery as John swept the wood cuttings into piles to be used as a binder in the plaster mud.

Once the wheelbarrow was emptied, Gareth lifted its handles for another trip to the woodpile and started down the hall to the servants' staircase. He came to Beth's chamber door and hesitated. Sleep had eluded him the night before, his thoughts returning again and again to Beth limp in his arms. Glancing hastily up and down the corridor and seeing no one, he pressed his ear to the polished wood. Nothing. No sound within. He drew back, shaking his head. The story Eleanore had told the previous night, and the news of Beth's grandparents' dreadful deaths would have sent anyone into a swoon.

John approached from behind, making Gareth jump. "Come," John said. "I'll join you in your wood gathering. Nicholas wants the wall patched up by day's end."

Gareth welcomed the help, as he had already made many trips on his own. He liked John's easygoing manner and work ethic, though he knew little about the man, only that he claimed to hail from two different counties, a detail which had sparked Gareth's curiosity.

Together, they returned to the courtyard, John insisting on pushing the wheelbarrow. The work went quickly with two pairs of hands. When they were done, Gareth motioned for John to sit on the remaining pile as he handed him a flagon of cold water.

Gareth glanced up at the granite sky. "There'll be rain come afternoon. Let's rest a spell and take in the cool morning air," Gareth said.

John gratefully accepted the leather pouch, took a long, hearty drink, and handed it back.

"I wish to thank you for helping us with our task," John said quietly, glancing about to ensure no one was nearby.

"Truth is, I had little choice. Lord Charles discovered my poaching." Gareth gave a rueful grin. "But if it keeps me from the gallows, it benefits us both."

"It benefits us all," John said earnestly.

"Those of the old faith, you mean," Gareth replied with a wink.

John lowered his gaze and said nothing.

"You told me you were from Derby," Gareth went on, changing the subject.

"That's right."

"I've family in Derby. Spent many summers there as a boy helping dig cockles along the coast."

John shifted uncomfortably. "Ah, yes, the Derby shoreline always provided a great bounty."

Gareth's expression darkened. "Except Derby has no coast, no shoreline, no cockles. It's landlocked, John. You lie."

John stared back at Gareth, wide-eyed, like a netted fish. Yet, instead of denying the claim, John stood and faced his accuser. "Come," he said. "I have something to show you."

Gareth followed John back through the servant's entrance and up the staircase. Instead of turning down the hall to the library, John continued to the apartment he shared with Nicholas.

Gareth hesitated. The silence between them was thick. He glanced back down the hallway toward the library. No one was in sight, but his boots felt rooted. "This better not be some trick," he muttered, then followed anyway.

The apartment door closed behind them, and Gareth stiffened as John slid the heavy bolt into place.

"Trust me," John said. "This will explain my deceit."

Despite John's words, Gareth remained on guard. These were dangerous times. He was lucky to have gotten away with fish thieving and was not keen on pressing his luck further.

A sideboard with a washbasin stood against the far wall. John removed the bowl and slid the narrow table across the floor before moving the carpet away. Underneath was a trapdoor. Pulling on the metal ring, he lifted the wooden cover, revealing a chest beneath the floorboards.

"Help me lift it out," he said, grabbing one end.

Gareth obliged with reluctance, and they both set the trunk on the floor. It was light and unadorned, about the size of a small merchant's trunk, but Gareth was quite certain its contents did not contain trinkets or herbal remedies.

When John opened the lid, the acrid scent of incense wafted from its contents.

On top of the trunk, carefully folded, was a garment of white cloth intricately embroidered with golden flourishes. John carefully moved the cloth and laid it gently on the sideboard. He unfolded it with reverence until the fabric covered the table, draping nearly to the floor. An unmistakable gold-stitched cross outlined in black appeared boldly on the front of the tapestry.

Gareth inhaled deeply. "What is this?"

"An altar," John replied evenly. His eyes were solemn. He held his arms out as if introducing himself for the first time. "I am a priest."

Gareth remained mute as John returned to the trunk and pulled out a chalice and serving plate, a leather-bound book Gareth guessed was a Bible, and a large metal crucifix held on a pedestal.

"I keep the most important relics for the Mass together. The other items are hidden away," John told him.

"Are you not afraid for your life?"

John shrugged. "I know no other life, nor do I wish to. My training began early at Bingham Priory in Norfolk, a Benedictine order. That is the only memory of my childhood. My parents placed me there in the monks' care when I was an infant. I think they hoped that offering my life to God would grant them an eternal one in heaven." He chuckled. "Apparently, being the youngest of twelve—I was expendable."

"I gather you saw little of Northumberland or Derby from behind those priory walls," Gareth added with a wry smile.

John shook his head. "Life within those walls was the only world I knew until now. Word came that the priory was to be seized by the queen and dismantled. A clever word to disguise the destruction that followed. Statues were destroyed. The stained glass was shattered. Everything of value was taken."

"I'm sorry," Gareth said. "It must've been horrible."

"I'll never forget what was done. Do you know the scent of frankincense never left the chapel?" John said, his voice trailing off. "Even after the shattering of the glass and the splintering of the pews . . . it lingered. Like a specter."

"What of the monks?"

"Most fled and live in hiding. Some stayed and were martyred. I was fortunate that Prior Geoffrey smuggled me off to Nicholas to continue our Lord's work, if only in secret."

Gareth marveled at John's courage. "You are braver than I could ever be. You were born to this, but I wasn't. When my money purse is full and the priest hole is complete, I will leave and be done with this place."

7

BETH

Beth's chamber door opened and softly closed, the bolt sliding into place. Lying beneath the heavy coverlet, she hastily closed her eyes and feigned sleep. She wished to remain there forever, entombed in the bed, not caring if she ever saw the sun or felt the dewy grass under her feet ever again.

Everything she thought she knew had unraveled. Truth and lies were blurred, and whoever stood beside her bed was not about to make things any clearer.

"Beth?" came Eleanore's gentle voice.

She clenched her eyes tighter, the ache in her heart beyond control. In her mind's eye, she saw them—two figures bound back-to-back, screaming amid the flames. She gripped the bedcovers, wishing the downy mattress would swallow her whole, burying her with a past too unbearable to endure.

Marge had divulged nothing about her grandparents. Neither had Peter. But they must have known. How could they not? And still, they had let her live in ignorance. Even as she lay there motionless, life pressed on like a surging tide, sweeping her along against her will.

"Beth," Eleanore said again, more urgently.

Reluctantly, Beth opened her eyes and peered over her shoulder.

Lady Eleanore had placed a tray with bread and a small mug that smelled of spiced tea upon the bedside table. It was strange seeing her mistress performing a servant's task. Ignoring the offering, Beth turned away and pulled the coverlet up once more.

"I'm sorry for your pain," Eleanore said, sinking down on the bed. "I meant to tell you the truth eventually . . ." She sighed when Beth gave no reply. "Time doesn't always grant the moments we hope for."

"You weren't looking to employ a scullery maid, were you?" Beth said with her back to Eleanore like a wall.

"That's true. But the news of Sarah's death presented an opportunity for us both."

"You needed someone to lie for you," Beth replied numbly. "To hold my past as hostage."

"I needed someone to entrust a secret to, and you needed a place to go."

Beth's eyes stung with tears hidden behind her lids; her pillow was still damp from the night before. Then she felt

Eleanore's hand press gently against her back. The tender touch, so unexpected, stirred a wave of longing she could neither welcome nor resist.

"There's more," Eleanore said. "Sarah spent her remaining days devoted to you, to your welfare, protection, your upbringing. She kept me apprised of your situation, as though her charity might mend what was broken between us." She paused, waiting, but again Beth said nothing. Silence settled like a heavy weight between them. "If my aunt could not undo the horror that had been done," Eleanore went on at last, "then I believe she sought, at the very least, to make some part of it right. I wish to continue that . . . if you'll let me."

The words rang hollow, but Eleanore's hand remained. Beth still did not answer.

"Yet I won't make you stay. You deserve to be happy. If you leave, you'll be given a dowry to use as you wish. Go where you will. You'll not face judgment." She paused. "But understand that you will always have a place here, if you want it."

Beth felt Eleanore's hand pull away as she stood. "For now, if you are up to it, I must ask that you attend to Master Owen. He has a cut that needs attention."

Beth heard Eleanore's gown swish across the floor, then the click of the latch. Although she wanted to bolt the heavy door and lay there forever, a few moments later, she tossed the coverlet aside and dressed.

She found Nicholas seated on a workbench, pressing his hand against his wounded arm to stave off the bleeding.

"It's not as bad as it appears," he said, his face flush with embarrassment as he showed Beth the cut. "I'd blame these old spectacles for failing me, but it was a slip of the hand. I fear they're not as steady as they used to be."

The wound was small but deep, and blood flowed again. Beth quickly removed several strips of fabric from her sewing basket and began binding the master carpenter's arm.

"There," she said, finishing the knot. "I will change the bandage again on the morrow."

"Thank you. I appreciate your kindness. Are you feeling well today? Lady Eleanore told me what happened last evening. Seeing Edward Hastings' punishment was a shock, I'm sure."

"As was learning the fate of my grandparents—and the connection between our mistress and the late Lady Sarah," Beth replied more harshly than intended.

"I know of their fate as well, Beth, and I'm very sorry. I shall pray for them and for you," Nicholas said, wincing as he shifted his arm.

She snapped the sewing basket shut. "My grandparents burned for their convictions . . . tortured in the flames by those who forced Catholicism upon the Protestants of England. Your religion is guilty of that. *You* are guilty of that!" An unquenchable fire raged within her chest. Anger surged like a great wave rising from the depths. "Now, I'm expected to help you and the Sheffields as though my family were of no consequence!" she spat.

"I am not a perfect man, Beth," Nicholas said quietly, "but that guilt is not mine. Every life is of consequence to me—even our queen, who persecutes Catholics, as Queen Mary oppressed the Protestants so many years ago."

His words softened her, and shame pricked her heart. Nicholas had shown her nothing but kindness. Deep somewhere inside, she knew this was not his burden to bear. "Forgive me if I am short-tempered," she stammered. "I am . . . overwhelmed."

Nicholas nodded and began unbuttoning his linen work shirt. "Only John and a few others have seen this. Perhaps it is important to show you, too."

Beth's breath caught as he revealed a chest covered in old scars, crisscrossing his skin like cruel brands. She turned away, remembering Edward Hastings and the inhumanity of a world that could be so cruel.

"The work of Protestant zealots when I was a young man," he said sadly. "Arrested with Edmund Campion, a Jesuit priest, whom I helped hide at Lyford Grange in Berkshire. They let me go, thinking I was a mere servant, unaware of who I really was. They tortured Edmund to death." He looked away and hastily buttoned his shirt. "Humanity has been abusing each other for their religious beliefs long before Queen Mary built her pyres, or our Queen Elizabeth installed the priest hunters. Her ladyship is not asking you to convert. They, as do I, ask that you aid us in hiding those who wish to perform their ministry for those who still practice and believe."

Beth listened attentively but was still unmoved. Nicholas's sad account did not change her present condition or bring her any closer to finding the truth about her own past.

"Come," Nicholas said, lightly taking her by the arm. "Let me show you what we're creating. It may soothe your heart or at least amuse you."

He led her to the wall next to the fireplace that had once held a built-in bookcase. A heavy work drape covered the wall from floor to ceiling. With his good arm, Nicholas pulled aside the cloth that concealed the work behind it. Despite days of construction noise, the unaltered wattle and timber wall startled Beth, appearing as if no one had touched it.

"I don't understand."

"Watch," Nicholas said and pushed a piece of the vertical timber panel. The wood see-sawed forward at the top, opening a crawlspace at the bottom. "Go on, look." His eyes danced with mischief.

Beth knelt and stuck her head inside the hole. As her eyes adjusted to the dark, a small cubby, roughly constructed, no bigger than a stool chamber, appeared before her. The space occupied the void between the bricked outside chimney wall and the library paneling, a cavern revealing the inner structure of the manor.

"There is still much work to be done. The floor still needs constructing, and the venting tested. Fresh air brought in somehow. And we must restore the library to its original state, of course. But when it is complete," he continued, "the wall will appear as it always did, a structure of plaster and timber that holds rows of books and . . ." He turned to Beth. "Forgive me. I forget myself."

Beth stood, and her hands caressed the timber as it fell back into place, looking again like an ordinary beam. "It is magic," she said, marveling at the secret entry. "You are quite an illusionist."

Nicholas beamed. "As a boy, I created puzzle boxes and admired the market performers with their sleight of hand and card tricks."

"The priesthood never called to you?"

"Carpentry is my life's ambition. My calling is to protect those who choose the priesthood."

"It is a fortunate thing to have found your place in this world, as dangerous as that place may be," Beth replied.

Nicholas rolled down his sleeve, preparing to return to his work. "Aye, danger can make us all leery of our calling and the journey toward what we hold dear. Yet, when we choose the mission, despite the perils, it is then we know the choice was a good one."

Beth set the water bucket on the rim-stones of the well and tied the thick rope to the wooden handle. She lowered it into the dark chasm below and waited for the echo of its splash. When the bucket was full, she turned the handle, winding the rope back onto the great spool until the bucket appeared, dripping in the pale morning light.

"Allow me," a voice offered from behind. Before she could answer, Gareth stepped forward, grasped the rope and pulled the bucket from the well, setting it on the ground between them.

"Thank you," she said softly, feeling his gaze upon her.

"Are you well?" he asked, with a measure of concern in his voice.

Beth blushed and nodded. "The news was a shock, of course, but I'll manage." She hesitated. "I must."

"We're in a precarious position, you and I. I almost regret poaching the lord's fish—almost." A mischievous grin tugged at his mouth, and the fleeting smile it drew from her seemed to please him.

"Despite what others have done, I'll do what's asked of me," she said and leaned in closer, her voice low. "I'm not sure I believe all of Lady Eleanore's tale. I need to know more. I mean to find the cook from Abury and learn the truth, as horrific as it may be."

"There is another truth that needs telling," Gareth said. "John is no mere apprentice. He's a priest—the one the Sheffields mean to hide."

Beth's eyes widened. "A priest? Already within the manor walls!" She drew a sharp breath. "Then he is not from Derby or Northumberland?"

Gareth shook his head. "He was a ward of Bingham Priory in Norfolk, destined for the cloth, but never ventured beyond its walls until the queen destroyed it."

She lowered her gaze and gave a slow, sorrowful shake of her head. "I never would have guessed John to be a priest. I hope he understands the danger he is in. He was not a witness to what we saw at Surrey." Beth's tone turned even more serious. "Do you trust them? Nicholas and John?"

Gareth leaned against the well. He brushed his bangs away and chuckled. "I trust very few, Beth, and I've only known them a short while. What about you?"

Beth inhaled deeply, swallowing her sorrow. "My world is turned upside down, and I live in a place with no family or friends. Only strangers—I trust no one."

Gareth covered his heart with his hand, feigning pain. "You trust me, though, don't you?" he said, sounding hurt. "I'm your friend."

Beth gave him a small smile, fighting the urge to laugh. "Thank you. Not only are you my first friend, but you are also my only friend."

Gareth returned her smile. "What of her ladyship?"

"What of her? She wishes me to stay even after Nicholas is done. Says I have a home here if I want it, and she means to grant me a dowry if I choose to leave. But where am I to go? What am I to do? I have no one." Just speaking the words made Beth's head swim.

"You mean she'd let you leave and give you a fortune besides?"

"Yes." Beth was unsure of why he sounded surprised.

"And yet, you're still here?" Gareth let out a long whistle. "I'd be far, far away from this place."

Beth stooped to pick up the water bucket. "I'm not going anywhere until I find Marge and Peter from my former home. They're the only people who know whether Eleanore speaks the truth. Once I speak with them, I will decide what to do."

A few days later, with Lady Eleanore's blessing, Beth set off for Surrey. Her ladyship insisted that a livery driver well-acquainted with the village streets, escort Beth. He introduced himself as Martin Winthrop, explaining, with a gleam of pride, that he had served the Sheffields as far back as Eleanore's parents. The man rode on top of the carriage, expertly handling the two spirited horses, while Beth traveled inside.

Beth had never ridden in such a fine carriage before. Plush bench seats faced each other, and the scent of leather lingered in the air. Two windows, open to the outside, flanked her seat, although she could draw the heavy velvet curtains closed to keep out foul weather and prying eyes.

Winter made an early appearance that morning, dusting the world in a thin veil of white. The muddy road to Surrey was mostly frozen, which lessened the risk of getting stuck in the mire. As they entered the village, the carriage slowed to a halt.

The driver turned and spoke loudly to her from his perch. He was an older gentleman, austere and formal, and looked dashing in his scarlet livery attire, trimmed in gold brocade. "Is there anywhere in particular you wish to go, miss?" he asked.

Beth did not know where to search for Marge. Her expression was one of uncertainty.

Sensing her uncertainty, the driver swung down from his seat and came closer to the window, his gloved hands resting on the frame. "Perhaps if you explain your purpose, I can be of better assistance."

Beth studied him, wondering how to broach the subject. She took a deep breath. "I am looking for the former undercook of Abury Hall. A woman called Marge."

Martin considered this before speaking. "As she's a cook by trade, taverns and inns would be the best places to visit," he replied matter-of-factly. "There are a few in this district, if you care to begin there."

"Yes, please. Thank you. I appreciate your counsel," she answered.

With a curt nod, he returned to his seat, and within moments, the carriage lurched forward again.

Despite the chill, Beth left the drapes open, eager to take in the village once more in all its chaos and wonder. The steady rhythm of the carriage slowed on the uneven stones as the press of villagers thickened and dwellings grew closer together, their timbered frames leaning into one another. It wasn't long before the carriage rattled to a stop, and the driver was at the window again.

"Here we are, miss." Martin gestured at a sign with a carved stag hanging outside the entrance of the building beside them.

Beth peered out the window for a better look.

The tavern was a solid two-story structure with a thatched roof. Smoke curled lazily from the stone chimney, carrying with it the scent of burning wood and roasting meat. Through the diamond-paned windows, the warm glow of light flickered, and muted laughter could be heard from inside.

Martin stepped forward and opened the carriage door. He presented his hand to assist Beth's exit.

"You may wait here," Beth said, leaving the carriage and straightening her cape. She preferred to handle the situation alone—particularly since she did not know how she would be received, nor how Marge would react to her questioning.

Martin shook his head and frowned. "Forgive me, miss, but I must escort you," he replied with a small bow.

Beth regarded him with a measured look and pondered who was really in charge, since they were both servants of the manor.

Guessing her thoughts, he added, "It is Lady Eleanore's preference, miss. I must do as I'm told."

Beth sighed and decided not to give the man any trouble. He'd been quite helpful thus far, and his guidance may still be needed. "Very well," she relented and accepted his arm, and together they entered the tavern.

As the heavy wooden door swung shut behind them, the scent of ale and spice filled the air. Long tables flanked with benches were arranged side by side. In the fireplace, a pig glistening with fat was skewered on a long, thick rod, slowly spinning round and round as the spit boy turned the handle. Lively patrons, laughing and chatting over food and drink, hardly noticed Beth and her driver.

Beth scanned the room, her eyes trailing the tavern's staff as they performed their duties. Seeing no sign of Marge, she approached an older woman by a side cupboard drying tankards. Martin dutifully followed, barely a step behind.

"Pardon me. Would you by chance have a woman named Marge in your employment?"

"No," the woman answered curtly, not looking up from her work.

Beth hesitated. "She may call herself Margery," she persisted, her eyes straining to see inside a storeroom behind the woman.

The woman gave an indifferent shrug. "No one by either name," she replied. Deep lines creased her face, and wisps of unwashed hair escaped the edges of her wimple.

Beth found it difficult to hide her disappointment. The woman's indifference chilled her. "She is the only family I have," Beth said quietly before turning to go.

For the first time, the woman's eyes flicked up at Beth. She set the dried cup on a shelf, then reached for another, but paused before Beth stepped away. "Is she new to the village? This Marge?"

"Yes." Beth stopped short, surprised.

The woman gave her a slow, wry grin, her teeth yellow with one missing from the bottom row. "Try the brothel. There's always work to be found there."

Beth inhaled sharply. Her mind swirled at the suggestion, but she thanked the woman anyway, reaching for her hand in gratitude. But the woman shirked away, as if Beth's touch might hurt.

"A brothel," Beth heard Martin murmur from behind. "Her ladyship will not be pleased, and my dear wife will like it even less." He sighed. "But I know where to take you."

They left the tavern and once more traveled the busy streets.

8

GARETH

The thin layer of morning snow caught Gareth unaware. Ordered to tend Nicholas's geldings before assisting in the library, he was grateful for the comfort of the stable. Its familiar smell of leather and whinnying horses was a relief from the construction and secrets elsewhere in the manor.

The priest hole had yet to be completed. Nicholas worked feverishly to finish the secret panel and hiding place while John and Gareth busied themselves replacing the library floor, creating enough noise and dust to avoid drawing attention to Nicholas's true task.

Still, Gareth could tell things had shifted. John was called away more often, leaving Gareth alone to gather supplies and lay out the heavy flooring. Villagers, poor and rich alike, began arriving at the servants' entrance at all hours, only to be led quietly down to the guest apartments and ushered away again just as discreetly.

It did not take Gareth long to understand that John's holy calling as a priest had begun.

Earlier that morning, Gareth had watched Beth step into one of his lordship's carriages and disappear beneath the arched gate displaying the Sheffield family crest and its motto "with God's help, there is nothing to fear" carved in stone, and his heart had quickened.

He liked to watch Beth as she worked, how she held a broom with a determined grip or the sway of her hips as she carried water. Her face was always serene, but her eyes held a faraway gaze, as if she were somewhere else.

He supposed she was traveling to Surrey to search for her people, and he sighed. Why couldn't she let the past rest? With the fortune offered to her, she could go any-where, be anyone, forge her own future unshackled by old specters. He would never understand the mind of a woman.

Gareth had just finished mucking out a stall when he heard a familiar voice behind him.

"Strange to find you back in the barn, Gareth. How goes your work with Master Owen?" Thomas leaned casually against the stall door, chewing on a bit of straw.

It had been several weeks since they'd last shared late-night banter and flagons of ale. Gareth missed his friend, yet since being assigned to the manor library, an uneasiness had settled between them.

"Very well," Gareth replied cautiously and wiped his brow, tossing the shovel aside. "Still have some of the floor to finish, but the lord and lady seem pleased."

Telling a lie to his friend was foreign to him, leaving a pit in his stomach, and he hoped Thomas did not notice the quaver in his voice.

"We miss you at the stables, the boys and I," Thomas said, crossing his arms. "Some lads think you've risen above your rank. That you think yourself better than us."

The comment startled Gareth. The thought of being talked about during his absence made him wary, and he gave Thomas a wry grin. "Sounds like those lads are envious. Is it because I smell more of wood shavings and less of horse dung? Are you jealous, too, Thomas? Is that what this is about? You know I am not one to shirk a duty. I obey orders, same as you."

Gareth did not mention that the duty not only paid handsomely but also broke the queen's penal rule against Catholics. Nor did he ask if Thomas had noticed the steady stream of visitors slipping in and out of the manor at all hours. Perhaps he had. Maybe Gareth wasn't the only servant to know the Sheffield's secret.

Thomas studied him for a long moment. "You're different somehow," he finally said. "You walk different. Speak different, too. Like you must be careful with your words, your actions. What happened to the Gareth I once knew?

You used to talk of leaving this place. Become your own tenant farmer. Or travel. Make your fortune."

"I still do," Gareth replied, reaching for a pitchfork to keep his hands busy. "My dreams are still in order."

Thomas glanced about warily and lowered his voice. "You no longer slip away and poach. Is your purse so full you've abandoned thievery? If only I had a coin bag so full . . ."

"My coin is none of your business," Gareth replied angrily and tossed a forkful of fresh straw into the corner. "Besides, how can I slip away with Lord Charles watching me around every corner?"

A wave of confusion and loyalty washed over him. He wanted to tell Thomas about the priest hole and the danger he was in, but it would only put his friend in certain peril and, besides, Gareth wasn't the only one who seemed different. Thomas's comments did little to hide his suspicion of Gareth. The days of their long, meandering talks and easy camaraderie were a distant memory. Now they spoke in warily in circles.

"I suppose you're right," Thomas answered, his jaw set firm. Then, as if deciding something, he tipped his cap, and his amiable smile returned. "I must be off. Take care, my friend," he said and turned to go.

Gareth watched Thomas disappear into the wintry morning. A knot tightened in his chest as he stabbed a bit of straw more forcefully than needed. Something was not sitting right, and he took a deep breath before slowly releasing it. Perhaps nothing would ever be right again.

Nicholas stood at his desk, head bent, deep in study over the parchment before him, the faint odor of burning beeswax and wood dust hanging in the air. Spread wide was a rough sketch of the angular shapes and shaded recesses of another priest hole.

Gareth set down the heavy bundle of planks and watched as the man carefully measured angles and distances, marking widths, scratching out lines and drawing out others. He marveled at the man's patience, his sharp mind and quiet devotion evident with every notch of the quill.

"You'll bore two holes in my back with that stare," Nicholas said, turning away from his draft, his voice calm but amused.

"Another priest hole, I see," Gareth said. "You have yet to complete this one. Still, you start another. Your work meanders like a spring stream from one project to the next. Do you ever tire of it, Nicholas?"

The carpenter rubbed his stubbled chin. "Hmm, I daresay I've never considered stepping away from my work, for it is never truly done. The Word of God depends on it. Priests like John depend on it."

Gareth nodded, unable to muster a smile.

Nicholas removed his spectacles and set them gently on the table. "What troubles you, Gareth? You are not yourself these days."

Gareth sat quietly for a moment, gathering his troubled thoughts. "Some things weigh heavier than bricks and timber," he said at last, staring at his calloused hands.

"And some burdens are not meant to be carried alone," Nicholas said, his voice soft yet firm. "What weighs on you so heavily?"

After so much time together, Gareth liked Nicholas. Even trusted the man. Perhaps it was best Nicholas knew the truth about his thieving past and troubled present.

Gareth stared at the wall that held the priest hole, wondering where to begin. "Did you know I was a thief?" he finally said. "I poached fish from the rivers right under the warden's nose. Sold them for coin, hoping to have a tenant farm one day." Gareth shook his head at the memory. "Strange, how I no longer steal, yet I feel all the poorer for it. I am bound to Lord and Lady Sheffield. Not just as a servant, but as a captive."

"How so?" Nicholas asked, crossing his arms.

"When his lordship discovered this theft, it was either the gallows or aid with the priest hole. Now Lord Charles pays me with his own coin. A bribe, of course, for my silence. Says I can be on my way once the work is finished." Gareth's tone saddened. "But the danger this work presents seems worse than the hangman's noose. It could bring ruin to many if discovered."

Nicholas tilted his head thoughtfully. "An old Jesuit once told me that the worst sin of all *was* theft." He lifted a hand as Gareth opened his mouth to object. "Everything can be stolen, you see," he continued, "not just coin or fish. But theft of happiness, of justice, character and dignity—even life."

Gareth stared at him with eyes full of challenge. "And what of me? You see only my labor. Fetching timber. Carrying mortar. What makes you so certain I'm not still that thief?"

"I've been here long enough to know you better than you think," Nicholas said quietly. "I've witnessed how you treat others—John and Beth, even your little dog. How you care in quiet ways. The respect you show even when you're weary. You're no thief, my friend. You may have stolen fish, but your heart is not a taking one. It is of giving. And as for danger, well, there are hazards everywhere. You can't out-build or outrun it. You can't pretend it isn't there. Some things, however, are worth the risk." Nicholas' lips spread into a wide grin as he slid his spectacles back onto his nose. "It is for you to decide what is worthy."

9

BETH

Beth and Martin stood outside The Black Swan, a brothel not far from the tavern. Nestled in a seedier part of the village, the building was larger than Beth had expected. The small second-floor windows were lit with flickering candles. Both men and women passed in and out with practiced ease.

"There are others," Martin said, nodding toward the brothel. "But this one has a reputation for fair pricing and cleanliness. A place, perhaps, where a cook might find work."

Beth digested the information in silence. She shuddered at the thought of how low Marge might have fallen from her former place at Abury Manor. The sadness of it settled heavily in her chest. If only the woman could return with her to Bodsworth. But the thought was fleeting. Life had taken them down separate roads; their destinies were no longer entwined.

Martin cleared his throat and looked down at the muddy road. "Please know that it has been a long while since . . . and I was a much younger and foolish man." He stared at his leather boots. "My wife would be heartbroken if she knew I was here."

Beth cut him short. "You need not explain anything to me, sir," she said curtly. "I am no one to judge anyone, and no one needs to know we were here."

Martin's demeanor softened with relief, and with a slight bow, he motioned to the entrance. "Shall we?"

Inside, The Black Swan bore a striking resemblance to the tavern. Long wooden tables and benches were crowded with patrons, drinking and laughing, and coins clattered onto tables as men played cards and dice. The air was thick with smoke and perfumed incense.

Yet, unlike in the tavern, women draped themselves on men's laps like ornaments, their bosoms spilling from unlaced bodices. Some allowed roving hands to stroke and tease, even reach up under their gowns. Beth caught herself staring and glanced away.

An older woman approached. She wore a gown of blue silk, a bit worn at the elbows. A string of pearls adorned her neck. She fluttered a bejeweled fan in one hand and held a velvet purse that jingled with coin in the other.

"The brothel-keeper," Martin murmured discreetly.

From her heavily powdered face, her dark eyes twinkled as she summed them up. "Welcome to The Black Swan.

I am Madam Wendland," she purred as her rouged lips spread into a wide smile. She glanced past Martin's dour expression and peered at Beth. "You are new to our fine establishment. We cater to many dark delights and can service any need, every desire—at a price."

Beth straightened her shoulders. "I come in search of a cook. A woman from the former Abury Manor. It's urgent that I find her."

Martin stiffened and coughed into his hand, and Beth feared she had misspoken.

Madam Wendland's eyes sharpened to a gleam. "This cook must be of great importance. Someone you love, perhaps? An older sister? Or your mother?" Her tone danced with the possibilities.

"Answer the girl," Martin growled.

"I have such a cook," she snapped back. "The price is a sixpence to speak with her."

Martin's eyes flew open. "Outrageous!" he exclaimed.

Beth's stomach sank. She lowered her gaze. "I don't have sixpence."

Without hesitation, Martin reached into his overcoat pocket and tossed two silver pieces into the woman's outstretched palm. "Bring out the cook," he told her with disgust.

Beth flushed with embarrassment. "Thank you. You are very kind. I promise to pay it back to you," she told Martin earnestly.

He didn't answer but locked his steely gaze on the brothel-keeper. Madam Wendland disappeared and quickly returned with Marge in tow. The woman—who had been more than a mother to her than anyone—halted in mid-step. Marge's mouth dropped open at the sight of Beth standing before her.

Beth's eyes welled with tears as she fought the urge to rush to her.

"Well?" Martin asked.

Beth bit her lower lip. "She is the woman I seek."

Madam Wendland clasped her hands together with exaggerated delight. "Excellent! A lovely reunion!" She turned to Marge. "This woman wishes to speak with you." Her tone turned sharp. "Don't be long. You have work to do."

Angry arguing broke out at a table where men were rolling dice, and Madam Wendland hurried away.

Beth took a step forward. "It's good to see you—" she started, but Marge quickly raised her hand, stopping her.

"Not here." She took Beth's arm and steered her toward a corner table away from curious ears and prying eyes.

They settled at the worn table, Martin standing dutifully behind Beth. His stern eyes assessed Marge with consternation.

The woman's eyes narrowed as she met his scrutiny with an amused grin. "No need to fret, good sir," she told him. "This may be a brothel, but I am still just a cook." She flashed a wry smile, and Beth found it hard not to laugh. Old Marge had not changed.

"I'm happy to have found you," Beth said awkwardly, as she searched for the right words to bridge the space between them.

"You sought me out," Marge replied, sounding pleased. "I hoped you might check on my welfare during these troubling times. You were always a thoughtful girl." She tilted her head slightly. "Are you faring well at Bodsworth?"

"I am," Beth assured her. "Though I am seeking answers to the troubling times—when I was a babe in your care."

Marge's eyes widened. She leaned back in her chair, crossing her arms. "Ah."

"Through Lady Eleanore, I learned my grandparents did not perish of plague," Beth said, her voice trembling. "They were put to the stake and burned." A lump rose in her throat.

Marge drew a long, uneven breath and exhaled slowly. "A terrible time," she murmured. "One I've no wish to remember." Her gaze fell to the worn floorboards.

Beth's pulse quickened. "But you must!" she cried, her voice rising enough to draw a few startled looks from nearby tables.

Marge glanced around the room, eyes wary, before meeting Beth's gaze again.

"Okay, okay. Hush now, girl," Marge said, leaning in until the candlelight caught the creases around her mouth. With her elbows resting on the table, she dropped her voice to a near whisper. "I was a young maid, new to the kitchen. Lady Sarah and Lord Thomas were strangers to me at first. I'd been tending the knot gardens with my sister. But fortune changed. God smiled on me, and I found myself working in the kitchen. And as time went on, I witnessed Lord Thomas's cruelty with my own eyes."

Beth leaned forward, meeting her stare, barely breathing as she listened. The clank of tankards and laughter faded into a distant hum. "What sort of cruelty?" she asked softly.

Marge swallowed. "He beat his dogs. That was the first sign. Then the spit boy took a terrible lashing for singeing a pig. I tended the boy myself." She closed her eyes for a moment. "Awful," she murmured. "But the worst was how he treated Lady Sarah—as though she were no more than a trinket. His to command. His to break. Not a wife, but a possession."

Marge's tale made Beth shudder. The kindly, gracious face of Lady Sarah had been nothing more than a mask to hide the pain of the past. "What of my grandparents," she asked, swallowing the lump in her throat.

"They were hardworking. Good folk. Both worked the fields. Your grandfather oversaw the plowing, the sowing, and the harvests. Lord Thomas trusted him. Your grandmother was also a proper healer. Good with herbs, teas, balms, and potions. Many benefited from her remedies—as did Lady Sarah. They became fast friends." Marge wagged a finger at Beth. "One night she sought out your grandmother when her husband refused to send for a physician."

"My grandmother restored her health?" Beth studied Marge's face, trying to connect the threads.

Marge grimly shook her head. "No, girl, your grandmother delivered her baby."

Beth sat back, stunned. "Lady Sarah had a child?"

"A boy."

"What happened to him?"

"Lord Thomas whisked him away that very night."

Beth's heart pounded. "But why?"

Marge's voice dropped even lower. "Don't you see? . . . it wasn't his. Lady Sarah had her secret ways, too. Locking herself away from prying eyes when Lord Thomas was off carousing. Given her husband's nature, I don't blame her."

Shock bolted through Beth. *Not his.* The words echoed in her head like a clanging bell. "You're certain?" she whispered.

Marge gave a slow, solemn nod. "I saw the babe. Light hair. Eyes like Sarah's. Not a trace of the lord in him. For a moment, I was happy for her. Happy that she had found a love all of her own—but she paid a heavy price."

Beth gripped the edge of the table. "Where did he take the child?"

"Lord Thomas left with a carriage and three riders. Said nothing to anyone. When he returned, he told Lady Sarah that the child had died in the night. She was hysterical, inconsolable. They buried an empty box the next morning."

Beth's mouth went dry. "And my grandparents?"

"Your grandmother confronted Lord Thomas," Marge said softly. "Condemned him right to his face in the great hall, no less. Demanded justice. Your grandfather stood by her. They were arrested a short time later by Queen Mary's inquisitors. Accused of being Protestant reformers and heretics. Lord Thomas made up the entire story to punish them and warn others who dared to cross him. I never saw your grandparents again until the day they were . . ." her voice trailed off.

Beth's heart pounded. "What of Lord Thomas?"

"Dead within a year," Marge replied. "Thrown from his favorite horse. Not even the physicians he once denied Lady Sarah could save him. He languished in bed for days with a split skull until the devil took him. No one was gladder to see him gone than her ladyship. It was as if a fog had lifted. Light cut through the darkness of that house." Her eyes brightened. "And then you came into her life—into all our lives."

Beth stared numbly at the table. "My grandparents were murdered. A child taken. Another orphaned. And no justice was done," she said numbly. A swell of emotions surged within her with no hope of release. Never had she been so lost, confused, and angry.

She blinked back tears as Marge reached across the table and took her hand. "Your grandparents were people of tremendous courage. Your parents were too. They carried your grandparent's memory with great strength. Folk at Abury never forgot, and when your parents succumbed to the sweating sickness when you were barely a yearling, there were many who wanted to take you in—Lady Sarah wouldn't hear of it. She insisted on taking you into her care, asking for my help." Marge swallowed hard, her eyes glistening. "There was never a greater honor for me."

Martin shifted uncomfortably as more angry words were exchanged nearby. "We must go," he said. "This place is no longer safe." Urgency tightened his voice. He was no young man, and Beth sensed he would be of little use if a brawl broke out.

Just then, Madam Wendland sauntered toward them with flinty eyes, jingling her money purse. If Beth wanted more time with Marge, more coin would be required, and she had none.

"Very well," Beth said to Martin and gave Marge's hand a last squeeze. "I will return to you. I promise."

Marge rose and moved to Beth with trembling arms. "Dear girl, I know not what trouble you face, but, as always, I pray for your deliverance."

A lump swelled once more in Beth's throat as she stood to meet her.

Madam Wendland swiftly stepped between them. "Displays of affection require further payment," she said, her eyes squinting at Martin.

Martin's hand slipped inside his coat pocket.

"No," Beth said firmly, her eyes locked on Marge. "Thank you for all you've done for me."

Marge smiled despite the tear that slipped down her cheek.

Beth and Martin turned to leave, Madam Wendland's voice trailing after them. "Not worth the price now, are you? Go on—back to the kitchen with you!"

Beth and Martin stepped outside onto the lantern-lit street just as the muffled crash of overturned benches and tables echoed behind them. She pulled her cloak tighter across her chest, warding off the cold and the hollow ache that settled in her heart.

Martin opened the carriage door, and as Beth reached for his outstretched hand, something caught her attention. She turned to see a cloaked figure quickly dodging her gaze, slipping down a narrow side alley, head lowered, face hidden.

She swung around toward the stranger as her heart quickened. "Who was that?"

Martin followed her gaze, brows furrowing. "Sorry, miss, I saw no one."

Beth made her way to the entrance of the alley, ignoring Martin's protests. A hint of metal lay in the mud, and she swiftly picked it up, wiping the grime on her cloak. It was a small crucifix meant to be hung on a chain. Beth turned it over in her hand. The metal was old and tarnished. She slipped it inside her pocket and returned to the carriage.

"Did you find something, miss?" Martin said, securing the door.

Beth pulled up her hood and leaned back against the seat, confused, cold, and exhausted. "Nothing of concern," she answered.

10

BETH

Beth stood in her bedchamber folding John's priestly garments, the door bolted. Her hand lingered on the fabric, which she had discreetly laundered the day before. Her finger traced the gold cross embroidered in the center.

The cross signified the same God worshipped and adored by all who claimed to be Christian. Yet, that very symbol cut the realm in two, drawing blood and suffering on both sides. Perhaps the cross itself was blameless. Maybe those who wielded the metal to suit their own purpose were the ones guilty of its defamation.

The pendant she had found outside the brothel lay hidden in her trunk behind a bit of loose lining. For the past several nights, sleep had escaped her. Her mind kept returning to the shadow figure, the cross left behind, and the certain, chilling feeling that someone had followed her. But why?

Beth brushed the uneasy question aside, scooped up the basket, and made her way to John's apartment. As soon as returning from Surrey days ago, she'd gone straight to Gareth eager to share Marge's tale of the lost child and the true reason behind her grandparents' death, while deciding it best not to tell him about the pendant or the stranger. The memory of his tender, quiet worry brought a smile to her lips.

As she passed Eleanore's den on her way, Beth halted abruptly. Raised voices carried through the closed door, loud enough to be heard in the corridor.

"You're certain, husband?" Beth heard Eleanore ask.

"A messenger came from court this morning," came Charles's reply. "The king of France is dead. And the Scots Queen—newly widowed—wastes no time rallying the Catholic nobles to her side. Says a Protestant heretic sits on the English throne—the throne she claims is rightly hers. The woman brazenly challenges her own cousin. It is treason, yes, but God bless her, what courage!"

Beth heard Eleanore draw a sharp breath. "No one denies that by birth her claim is strong. The kingdom may yet return to Rome and Pope Pius. Still, like her father, our queen has a lion's heart. What does she propose to stop the uprising? We have no standing army."

"Our virgin queen has a suitor," Charles responded, his lowering voice making Beth take a step closer to the door.

"An ardent one, at that—King Philip of Spain. He offers his hand and his Spanish army to crush the rebellion."

"The offer must come at a price. What does he seek in return?" Eleanore asked.

There was a long pause before Charles answered, "Queen Elizabeth must abandon her Protestant faith. Convert to Catholicism."

Eleanore's voice rose to an excited pitch. "There is no way out for her then! If she refuses, she loses her throne. If she accepts, England returns to the true faith. Perhaps the priest hole and all we've accomplished were for naught."

Charles's voice sounded certain. "Nay, returning to the true faith is a good thing. A blessing. To worship openly once more. Bring back the sacraments and saintly statues. Perhaps even rebuild the abbeys, churches and cathedrals. I'd gladly brick up that priest hole myself to see the realm back in Rome's good graces."

A floorboard creaked and Beth spun around, heart thudding, to find Kat sidled up behind her in the dim hallway.

"Spying on the lord and lady, are we?" Kat hissed, a smug glint in her eyes.

Beth straightened, struggling to mask her alarm. "What are you doing here?" Her voice wavered despite herself, brittle with fear.

Kat held a bucket of soot on her arm. "Doing your work again. You're falling behind, sweet Beth. I wonder what his lordship would say if I told him what I saw. Perhaps I'd be rewarded. Maybe you'd be doing my work instead."

"I am no spy," Beth said quickly, heart hammering in her chest. "You startled me—I was just about to knock," Beth said. It was a flimsy, desperate lie, but it was all she could think of.

Kat's smile was knife-thin. "Is that so? Let's see if your claim is true." She reached around Beth, rapped sharply on the door three times, and, with a triumphant smirk, scurried away, the soot bucket swinging.

For a moment, Beth's only thought was to run, escape to an empty bedchamber, vanish into the scullery, hide in the laundry or a stool chamber until the storm passed. Perhaps it was too late for that. Perhaps fleeing would give Kat more power, more ways to make her miserable and afraid.

Before she could choose, Eleanore's voice beckoned and, with no choice but to obey, Beth opened the door and went in.

Eleanore and Charles sat opposite each other in matching high-back chairs, cozy and warm from the fireplace's glow. The scent of mulled wine hung in the air. Each held a goblet, and their flushed cheeks suggested the enjoyment of more than one glass.

"What brings you here, Beth?" Eleanore asked. Her gaze was steady, one eyebrow arched.

Beth's mind scrambled for an answer, and her tongue felt thick in her mouth. Then she remembered her laundry basket.

"I—I am delivering fresh garments to Master John, my lady," she stammered. "I knocked at your chamber mistakenly. It was foolish of me."

Eleanore's eyes flicked to Charles and then back to Beth. "I would have thought you'd learned your way about the manor by now," she said.

Beth swallowed hard. Was this a test? Had Eleanore and Charles heard the squabble with Kat outside the door? Her skin prickled with heat.

Charles turned from the fire. His eyes were sharp despite the flush in his cheeks. "No harm done," he said smoothly. "Go. Deliver your linens. When you see John, tell him and Master Owens we wish to speak with them both." He paused, his brows furrowed. "And, Beth ...be sure of your way. The matter is urgent."

⚜

When Beth entered the library, she found it empty. Neither Nicholas, John, nor Gareth was anywhere to be seen. Coals smoldered in the hearth, and Nicholas's drafting quills stood neatly in the inkpot.

Cautiously, she made her way down the corridor to Nicholas and John's apartments, wary of Kat around every corner. As she approached the door, voices drifted from within. She softly knocked and entered as she had done many times before, expecting familiar faces.

Instead, three surprised expressions greeted her. John and Nicholas stood tense. Between them, a bearded stranger swiftly stepped back. The man was Nicholas's age. He wore a loose-fitting robe cinched at the waist with a braided cord, and a band of graying hair remained above his ears, while the rest of his head was shaven.

Beth stood silent as John moved to close the door left open behind her.

"No cause for alarm, Beth," Nicholas said, composing himself. "Rowan is a friar seeking sanctuary for the night." He rested a comforting hand on the man's shoulder. The gesture did little to console him; Rowan's tired eyes, wide with fear, darted nervously about the room.

"I will go," Rowan said. "The risk is too great."

"Nonsense," John replied. "You'll eat and sleep and be well-rested for your journey to Scotland on the morrow."

"The Highlands will welcome you as a fellow Catholic, brother," Nicholas added.

Rowan studied Beth's work dress and apron. "The girl is but a servant. Can she be trusted?"

Nicholas nodded his head in earnest as he turned to meet Beth's anxious gaze. "Yes, Beth is a good and loyal friend."

"What brings you here?" John asked her. "Is there something you need?"

Beth dipped a quick curtsy. "Our lordships request both your presence in the lady's den."

"Very well," Nicholas said. "We won't delay. While we're gone, please see that Rowan has food and drink."

A short time later, Beth returned with cheese, bread, and a mug of ale. Rowan accepted the offerings with gratitude, his fear yielding to the demands of an empty stomach.

Beth watched as he tore into the bread, swallowing large bites between gulps of ale.

"'Twas a blessing you escaped the priest hunters," she said softly, her thoughts turning to the Montgomery family and Marge. "I fear for those who remain under their scrutiny."

Rowan's voice dropped low. "Trust is a scarce commodity among the village folk. They smile, bid each other 'good day,' yet suspicion festers beneath. Some serve the priest hunters, no matter the cost. Bayne and Holbrook—aye, they're relentless in their pursuit." He took a large swallow of ale. "Bayne most of all. He despises not only the faithful, but mankind itself. His cruelty . . . it is not of this world."

Beth inclined her head in quiet assent. "I've witnessed his evil handiwork myself," she said. "He is the reverend's hound."

Rowan scoffed. "A hound obeys his master. Bayne is no hound, but a wolf in royal garb." He pressed a hand to his chest and lowered his eyes. "Shame eats me to the core."

"Shame?"

"I flee to Scotland—to safety—while others like Nicholas and John stay and endure. It is through them that the faith is kept alive."

"Staying alive also keeps the faith. Does it not?" she asked. "You'll bring hope to others."

He gave a faint, weary smile. "That is what I tell my-self. That I'll carry the truth across the border. But in my dreams I hear the cries of the persecuted—the crack of the whip. The screams of those left behind. And I want nothing more than to shrug off this cassock and become someone else."

Beth thought again of her grandparents, of firelight against the dark sky, the scent of smoke and ash.

"I understand," she said quietly. "I do."

"I don't mean to burden you."

"I am not burdened," she assured him, then added, "and I will bring you layman's clothing."

When they arrived back from Eleanore's den, Nicholas and John's faces were flushed with the news overheard by Beth.

"Don't you see?" John said to Rowan excitedly. "You may stay now. It won't be long until the Scots queen overthrows Elizabeth, and Catholics may step from the shadows at last."

Rowan turned away, rubbing his temples. "And you believe this news?"

"It is said the queen's very life is in danger. Her guards watch her constantly. Even her food is tasted," John replied, a flash of hope in his eyes.

Beth grasped the edges of her apron, grounding herself in place. The familiar swell of fear rose in her gut. *What if John was wrong? What if such rumors only fed the hunters' fury?*

Nicholas held up a hand and shot John a warning look. "The news is good, yes, but let's continue our course and pray the news will bring our deliverance," he said, tempering John's enthusiasm. "I have spoken to our lordships, and they have agreed that Rowan may stay, but we must move with caution."

"I will draw suspicion," Rowan said, his voice low and urgent. "If they find me, they'll not stop with me. You, the girl—the entire household—will be strung up for harboring a heretic."

Nicholas shook his head. "You are a laborer at my request. A very reasonable explanation. Besides, the lord and lady demand it."

Then, a soft knock rattled the door. All heads turned as another wave of fear rushed over Beth.

A short blade swiftly appeared from beneath the sleeve of Rowan's robe as another knock came.

"Beth," a voice called softly.

She let out a grateful breath. "It's Gareth," she told the others.

Rowan's knife disappeared under the cassock's folds as Beth eased the door open.

Gareth stood in the hallway with a rolled feather bed across his shoulder. He strode across the room to the hearth and laid the bundle on the floor. "From Lady Eleanore for the new laborer," he said, sizing up the man. Gareth's wide eyes settled on Beth with a look of suspicion, and she answered with her own look, telling him all was well.

Beth felt the tremor in her hands dispel slightly. There was still fear, yes—but also purpose. She was no longer a mere bystander. As the world shifted beneath her feet, she had chosen her place.

"Let's return to work," Nicholas said. "There is still much to be done." He looked at the friar and nodded at the work clothes Beth had delivered. "Change your clothes, and Beth will bring you to the library. For now, you are no longer Rowan, a friar of the Franciscan order, but Simon, a carpenter from the village."

11

BETH

Beth entered the library with a pitcher of ale and mugs. She set down the tray on a corner table and surveyed the pile of lumber yet to be laid. The priest hole was completely hidden. No one would guess what lay beyond the bookcase wall. Nicholas stood at his desk, engrossed in drafts, while Gareth and Rowan—now Simon—hammered the floor planks back into place, the floor still only half restored.

"Simon the carpenter," she said under her breath, filling the mugs with ale. The lie seemed strange on her lips.

The man, having removed his robe and cord belt, wore a simple tunic and work breeches. The transformation was miraculous. Though the beard and eyes still belonged to a man of God, the new clothes recast him in an entirely different light—a simple carpenter, humble and modest.

Awaiting news of the Queen of Scots' uprising was unbearable. Information swayed from better to worse, like the bell knocker swinging in the chapel tower. Tales of battles won and lost turned out to be only civil disturbances between Mary Stuart's Protestant and Catholic nobles and her inability to rule over either of them.

Without a word, Beth left the men at their work and headed to the great hall. The twelve days of Christmastide were upon them, and there was much work yet to be done. The season marked the birth of Christ and a time of merriment, feasting, and reverence.

As she entered the hall, the scent of pine and rosemary lingered in the air. Boughs of greenery adorned the hall's rafters and candelabras. Moving swiftly, servants arranged garlands of ivy and holly on the long trestle tables as others polished cutlery and arranged trenches. They placed a yule log, more tree than log, near the hearth, having stripped it of branches, preparing to light it on the morrow, Christmas Day. Its fire was meant to last until the twelfth day, the last day of Christmastide.

Beth joined the other maids, dusting benches and placing ewers along the sideboard. Her hands moved deftly through the familiar motions, but her thoughts remained with the men in the library, particularly Rowan, and how long the ruse would last.

"Doesn't seem right celebrating while the queen's men keep the village under siege," Beth heard a maid say under her breath.

"Houses ransacked. Many arrested. There are whispers of torture, too. I'm told they even question children. Pressed into giving up their family," another mumbled sadly.

Beth swished her rag along the polished bench, keeping her eyes low. "Have they found more priests?" she asked casually.

The girl to her left paused and leaned closer. "No. But yesterday, a friar narrowly escaped capture at the smithy. They arrested the owner of the shop."

Beth clenched the rag tightly as her stomach recoiled. George Montgomery—taken. The iron-willed blacksmith, whose only crime was loyalty to his family and neighbors, was a captive.

She swallowed hard. "Where did they bring him?" she asked lightly.

The other girl shrugged. "No one knows. He was a fighter, though. They say he didn't go easily. One guard got a broken nose for his trouble."

There was a small, admiring chuckle from one of the older women. "Aye, that sounds like George."

Beth found no relief in George's refusal to back down. Bravery would not save the man from interrogation, the rack, or the pyre's flames. George's stubbornness would only make Bayne and the reverend more determined in their cruelty.

Hastily, she excused herself, murmuring something about retrieving linens. Once out of sight, she gathered her skirts and broke into a swift stride, not stopping until she reached the library.

All three men looked up from their work as Beth barged into the room, breathless and shaken.

"They've taken your father," she said to Gareth in quick gasps. "They say he resisted—at the smithy. Was harboring a friar who escaped . . ."

Silence fell over the room.

Gareth's jaw tightened, and his hands balled into fists at his side. "They'll torture him."

Rowan rose, pale and stricken. "This is my fault. I never should have gone there." He turned to Gareth. "Forgive me. I didn't know he was your father."

"There is nothing to forgive," Gareth replied swiftly. "Fault lies with the queen and her men. Nowhere else."

"We must act quickly," Beth said. "Who knows where they've taken him!"

"We must tell our lordships," Nicholas reasoned.

Gareth's eyes flashed with anger. "You think I need permission to save my father?" he countered. "I leave now!"

"I'll go, too," Beth said, meeting his steady gaze.

Gareth shook his head and took her hands in his. Her heart thudded against her chest. "No, Beth. Stay. Both of us being gone will raise suspicion. Besides, the queen's men may recognize you. You'd be taken too."

"As they will surely recognize you!" she cried.

"They won't know me," Rowan claimed with certainty. "I escaped the village before they laid eyes on me. I'll travel as I am—Simon—a simple laborer." He turned to Gareth. "Your father came to my aid when my trouble was great, despite not sharing the same faith, and I will do the same for him."

Gareth answered with a slight nod. "And I can lead you back to the village along the paths that don't show on any map."

Nicholas rubbed his forehead. "Reverend Holbrook won't keep your father in the village long. You must get to him before they move him to a holding post, or worse, London." He turned to Beth. "Can you keep things quiet while this plan is carried out? It may be a few days."

Beth nodded. "If anyone asks, I'll say Gareth has taken ill. That he is resting until after the Christmastide banquet on the morrow."

"Very good," Nicholas said.

"Anything else?" Beth asked, eager to help, if only from afar.

Nicholas's eyes were solemn. "Pray."

That night, Beth met Gareth behind one of the larger cow sheds. Blackthorne stood saddled, pawing at the gravel with impatience. Dressed in a dark, hooded riding cloak with a dagger attached to his belt, Gareth cinched the saddle girth one last time.

Beth handed him a sack of food and a flagon of water. He peered inside the sack and gave it back to her, keeping the water.

"Thank you, but no," he said. "I must travel light."

"At least take this," she said and pressed a small pouch of coin into his hand. "From my dowry . . . money for bribes or whatever else you may need."

The thought of Gareth leaving, perhaps never to return, made his departure even more unbearable. She had grown used to his ways, his moods and mischievous smile. Yet, if not now, someday when the priest hole was complete and his money bag was full, Gareth was destined to leave for good and follow his dream anyway. It was best to remember that, she chided herself silently.

Gareth's expression softened. "You are kind, Beth," he said, "and I will tell my father of your bravery." He reached for her hand, holding it a moment longer than necessary before slowly letting it go.

Tears gathered in the corners of her eyes, but she held them back.

A gust of wind stirred Gareth's cloak as he climbed onto Blackthorne's back. "Rowan will meet me at the brook within the hour. We thought it best not to leave the manor together."

Beth swallowed a lump in her throat and forced a nod, ready to watch him go, but a rustling then a shadow caught her attention, and for a moment Beth thought they were discovered.

Gareth held the reins tight as Blackthorne danced nervously at the sight of the stranger.

"Wait! It is only me," John whispered, pulling his priestly cowl down from his head. "I am here to offer a blessing."

"For heaven's sake, John!" Beth scolded. "Why didn't you tell us you were coming?"

"Sorry, a villager seeking confession detained me. But I couldn't let Gareth leave without a prayer."

"Very well, but hurry," Gareth said, agitated, stroking Blackthorne's neck to settle him.

John laid his hand on Gareth's knee and bowed his head as he prayed for safe passage and a favorable outcome.

When he had finished, Beth stepped back. Gareth gave her one last look before Blackthorne circled and disappeared into the dark night, the steady rhythm of hooves fading into silence.

When he was gone, Beth offered a silent prayer of her own—not just for clear roads and God's protection, but for Gareth to return to her whole and well.

As she headed back to the manor with John, neither of them saw the figure watching from behind the hedgerow near the path, still as stone.

The next day was Christmas Day, the first of twelve days for feasting and revelry and to set work aside. Tenants gathered in the courtyard, ready to be received for the banquet in the great hall. It was the fourth time during the year that the villagers mingled and gathered with the manor nobles to share a grand meal and to celebrate.

Beth mustered a smile when Annie complimented the crown of ivy woven through her braided hair.

"What is it, girl?" Annie said, her face already rosy from manor wine. "It's Christmastide!"

"And happy Christmas to you," Beth said with a small curtsy. Eager to avoid more conversation, she lifted a platter and followed the other servants as the guests filed into the hall.

The scent of roasted meats, sugared nuts, and fresh bread mingled with the pine and smoke from the yule log blazing in the great hearth. Tenants and local merchants wandered amongst the long benches, marveling at the tables laden with steaming pudding, roasted pheasant, and stacks of honey cakes. Sconces burned brightly, casting a golden glow upon the swaths of green garland and red-berried ivy. Weeks of unease and scrutiny under the priest hunters gave way, at least for the night, to laughter and good cheer as everyone took their seats.

The banqueters rose as Lord and Lady Sheffield entered, Charles's velvet-trimmed doublet matching Eleanore's elegant crimson gown. Murmurs and whispers rippled through the hall as the men who followed them drew every gaze. Trailing in the Sheffields' wake came Holbrook and Bayne.

Beth nearly dropped the plate in her hands. A jolt seized her chest as the two men's eyes swept the room with practiced scrutiny. Dressed in black, the two men stood in stark contrast to the cheerful colors of the guests and the festive glow that filled the great hall.

Beside her, a maid whispered, "Christ have mercy."

Beth put down the tray and pressed herself against a pillar for support, her breath quick and shallow. *Were they here for Gareth? Had Rowan been found out? Was George's rescue in peril?*

As the foursome took their places upon the dais, Lord Sheffield raised a goblet. "On this blessed day, we thank Almighty God for the gift of life. We are grateful for the bounty we gladly share with our tenants and good neighbors, and . . ." He cleared his throat. "Her Majesty's retinue—Reverend William Holbrook and Sir Richard Bayne—honor us with their presence. Eat, drink, and may joy rule the day."

A strained applause followed, and the crowd began passing platters of goose, venison, and mince pies down the tables. Wine flowed, and no cup sat empty for long. A roasted boar's head, reserved for the lordships, was carefully placed on the dais table. Sugared fruit shimmered around the beast's golden tusks like jewels.

Bayne did not sit. He lingered at the hearth, his eyes roving the hall like a hawk trained to strike. Holbrook said something to Eleanore, who replied with a thin, careful smile.

An usher came up beside Beth. "Here," he said, handing her a tray with a wine goblet. "Bring this to Sir Bayne."

Fear gripped Beth. Catching Bayne's eye was not what she wanted. Surely, he would know her, remember her from the road or the fight at the smithy.

"Make haste, girl!" the man barked.

Beth forced herself to take the tray, steadying it as best she could. She wove slowly through the stream of servers, delaying the moment until the weight of Bayne's glacial stare was upon her. His eyes seemed to flay skin from bone.

Lowering her gaze, she curtsied and offered him the drink.

He took it, and Beth turned to go. A small sigh of relief escaped her.

"Wait," Bayne ordered.

Beth stiffened. She turned back to face him. His eyes narrowed.

"Your name eludes me. What is it?"

"Beth, sir," she answered. Her voice felt thin as a flush rose to her cheeks.

He swallowed some wine, his gaze unmoving. "From the smithy. A friend of the Montgomerys." His tone was curious—too curious. His eyes held an uncomfortable glint as they drifted from her face to her bodice and lingered.

"Just a servant girl," she replied hastily.

"A friend nonetheless," he said, finishing the wine in one mouthful. "Where is the blacksmith's son? His father's been arrested."

"Quite ill, sir. Kept away from the festivities for safety's sake."

"Then I'll wait until he's well to question him," Bayne said, the corner of his lip curling into a smile. "In the meantime, you'll do. Come to my chamber this evening for questioning." He placed the empty glass back on the tray and waved her away. "Go."

Beth forced herself forward. She placed the tray on the nearest table with care and retreated to the servants' alcove where Annie was ushering out trays and dishes.

"I'm unwell," she told the undercook, placing her hand across her stomacher for effect.

Annie studied her face. "I knew something was amiss," she said and touched Beth's cheek with the back of her hand. "No fever, but you are flushed. Well, nevertheless, go to your chamber until you feel well enough to return."

Beth bowed her head and hurried down the corridor and up the servants' stairs, making her way to the library hall. She hadn't traveled far when Nicholas and John rounded the corner, their faces stricken with panic.

"Holbrook and Bayne are here!" she cried hastily.

"We know," John answered, his face pinched with worry. "But something has happened. We must get to the stables quickly."

Beth could not fathom what could be more perilous than the arrival of the queen's men. "Tell me!" she demanded.

Nicholas raised a hand to quiet her. "Tomorrow is the Feast of Saint Stephen," he said, his voice low.

Beth stared back blankly.

"He is the patron saint of horses," John explained. "When the saints were celebrated, priests decorated and blessed the horses. A stable lad just left us. He was looking for Gareth. He found one of the lord's geldings a short time ago covered in ribbons and beads."

"Someone knows the Sheffields are Catholic loyalists!" Beth said under her breath, her head swimming. "The stable boy—does he know of this tradition?"

"No. But if he speaks of it, even out of ignorance, it will be enough to rouse suspicion. Worse, if the horse is found, it will be taken as proof," Nicholas said grimly.

John shook his head. "Where are Holbrook and Bayne now?"

"In the great hall feasting," Beth replied.

Nicholas shrugged on his overcoat. "Good. We may have time before the horse is discovered. Come along. We'll need your help."

They hurried to the stable, taking care to avoid revelers stumbling about from too much drink. Inside the great stone barn, the smell of hay and leather did little to settle Beth's nerves. Gareth's absence loomed large; a comforting presence that was sorely missed.

The threesome hurried down the center aisle, checking each stall as they went.

"There," John suddenly said, pointing.

In the last stall, a gray-dappled gelding stood covered in red and white ribbons. Beads and small silver bells were plaited throughout its thick mane, and a garland of evergreen hung around its neck—meant as a blessing, now a curse.

"Dear God," Beth whispered. "It's true. Someone wants to expose the Sheffields."

Nicholas glanced at her, breathing hard. "Perhaps us along with them, I fear."

John moved quickly, yanking the garland away, and Nicholas untied the beads and bells, as Beth grabbed a grooming brush to tug off the ribbons.

When they were finished, John slung a small sack filled with adornments over his shoulder. "I'll burn it all in the fireplace tonight," he said.

Beth nodded, relieved no one had discovered them, but her eyes welled with tears.

John lightly touched her arm. "What is it, Beth?"

Unable to help herself, she told the men about the meeting planned with Bayne.

Nicholas exhaled sharply and shook his head. "That demon has more on his mind than mere questions."

John turned to her, his expression grave. "We won't let it happen," he said, his voice firm.

Beth managed a faint smile, the weight in her chest easing just a little. She had been wrong about not having friends. Gareth was not her only ally. The knowledge settled warm in her belly, a quiet comfort that tempered the storm of fear.

"Thank you," she said. "Now go on without me. I'll see you back at the library, but first I'll check the tack room. There may be other traces left behind."

The men agreed and departed.

While the manor's groomsmen continued to feast, Beth cautiously entered one of the smaller tack rooms near the stable entrance. Rows of saddles lined the walls, while bridles and harnesses hung neatly from hooks.

Beth stepped lightly, her eyes scanning every surface. Finding nothing, she moved to the far end of the room where the saddle pads and polishing rags were neatly folded and stacked on a shelf. As she carefully lifted the fabric, a thin piece of red ribbon peeked out from the cloth, catching her eye. She pulled the strip from under the fold. It was long, probably meant to adorn a tail or mane, and it was the same color red as seen on the gelding.

"Who did this?" she whispered to the still air.

The sound of pounding hooves entering the stable yard ended her search, and she quickly slipped the ribbon inside her apron pocket. Her mind raced trying to think of an excuse before being discovered, but fear overtook her, and she hastily squirmed behind a grain barrel.

The door swung open, and Gareth stepped inside, leading Blackthorne.

"Gareth?" Beth stepped out from her hiding place, heart quickening, startled to see her friend so soon.

He lifted his head slowly. His eyes were hollow, ringed with exhaustion. Wind had tossed his hair into disarray, and grime smudged his cheek.

"Beth . . ." his voice cracked, raw and brittle.

A chill swept through her as she hurried to him. "What happened? Where's your father?"

Gareth's eyes swelled with tears as his face twisted with grief. "Gone," he answered faintly and let go of Blackthorne's reins as his knees buckled.

Beth tried to catch him, and they both sank to the dirt floor. He collapsed against her, sobbing into her shoulder. *Gone.* The word echoed back to Lady Sarah's death not so long ago, how she had slipped away, vanishing in death's grip during the night.

She clutched him tightly until the flow of sorrow ebbed enough for him to speak.

"We found him at Briargate, a garrison not far from Surrey. Rowan bribed the watchman. He led us to my father's cell. I hardly recognize him. They'd . . . they'd done things. Brutalized him. He was weak, with hardly a breath left in him. But he smiled when he saw me."

Beth squeezed his hands.

Gareth looked down at their interlaced fingers and gripped hers tighter. "He was proud of me, Beth. He said so. Told me I had every right to choose my path. That he just couldn't bear to see me leave . . . and now he's gone." His jaw trembled, and Beth kept hold of his hands, steadying him. "Rowan prayed over him and wept with me as he drew his last breath. Then the watchman ordered us to leave while the guards were still drunk."

Beth's throat burned as she tried to find words. "You did all that you could," she said, the words ringing hollow even to her own ears.

"I can't even take his body home to my mother. Bury him properly. There was no time . . ." His body shook as his sobs overcame him again.

Beth embraced him, and they stayed that way for a long while on the cold earth until his shaking stilled.

Finally, he drew a breath and stood, reaching down to help her rise, his palm warm in hers. He wiped his mouth with the back of his hand. "They'll pay for what they've done! God help me, Beth, they'll pay!"

12

BETH

Beth had already retired to her chamber when the summons came. Bayne was waiting for her in the downstairs parlor. Dread curled in her stomach. She clutched the edge of the washstand, recalling Gareth's hurried words after he'd spoken to John and Nicholas. *Worry not . . . a plan has been laid.* But now, alone in the silence of her room, that vow felt distant and fragile.

Arriving at the parlor door, Beth dug her nails into her palm and knocked softly on the dark wood.

His command to enter came quickly, as if he'd been kept waiting, and when she stepped into the room and saw his brow thick with sweat and his eyes bloodshot from too much drink, her gut twisted.

The queen's men had overtaken the richly decorated room once reserved for leisure. Stacks of documents were arranged in orderly towers on carved oak tables. More papers and leather-bound books crowded the gaming tables.

Inquiries of the accused, Beth thought bitterly, and she wondered if George Montgomery's bloody account was among the pages.

Bayne reclined in a high-backed chair near the hearth, legs splayed, a wine goblet teetering in his hand. Seeing Beth enter, he raised himself up as if his weight pained him and beckoned her closer. Behind him, the fireplace flames cast a daunting silhouette of his broad shoulders and tall stature.

Beth swallowed hard. "You summoned me, sir?" she asked, her voice small.

His lip curled. "You need not be afraid," he said, approaching with a stagger. "I mean no harm."

Beth's gaze dropped to the hearth, where sharp metal tools were grimly displayed. A chill ran through her. Had her friends failed her?

Bayne leaned closer and brushed a damp strand from her face, his hand lingering too long on her warm cheek. "Instruments of interrogation reserved for those with knowledge," he murmured. He cupped her face with both hands, diverting her eyes away from the hearth and back to his. Beth stiffened. The foul stink of wine and sweat clung to him. Her eyes burned with tears. "You, though, are no conspirator . . . just a frightened little hare. Not a threat to anyone, really. No," he whispered close to her ear, his voice thick with desire. "What you have is something far more interesting to me."

"Please don't . . ." she begged, squirming, as his arm curled around her, pulling her in.

"Do you think I rose to this position by folly, girl?" Bayne's grip tightened. "Actions are rewarded when commands are followed. Never questioned—no matter how bloody. Reformers. Papists. Neither matters to me. I'll always be on the side that rewards me best." His fingers fumbled with her bodice laces. "Now it's time for another prize. One that is sure to be quite pleasing."

A heavy knock echoed on the door, and Beth willed herself to not cry out for help. Bile rose in her throat as she said a silent prayer for deliverance.

But it was not Gareth whose voice followed

"Sir Bayne!" came a welcome voice from a guard. "Summons from Lord Charles. You're wanted in his private den."

Bayne growled under his breath. "Tell him I'll come when I please!" he bellowed, tightening his grip around Beth's waist.

A pause, then the voice returned, firmer this time. "He said now, sir."

Bayne released Beth with a shove. "Go! But remember . . . I'm not through with you!"

Beth stumbled back, landing on the cold tile, as Bayne stormed past her and out the door.

Moments later, Gareth burst into the room and dropped to her side. "Are you alright? Did he hurt you?" His hands hovered over her, his eyes blazing with fury.

"He did me no harm," she said shakily, brushing dust from her apron.

His gaze swept her face, frantic. "I don't believe you! First my father—now you! That bastard will pay for everything he's done, and I'll be damned if he ever lays a hand on you again!"

"Truly, I'm not hurt," Beth replied, her voice trembling. "Bayne was called away before anything happened." Her eyes brimmed with tears, and she looked away. "I thought you'd never come . . ."

Gareth drew her into his arms and held her close. "I'm sorry. Annie sent me to find Master Benjamin in the wine cellar to choose a barrel. Then a messenger arrived from court—news spread that the Scots Queen had been arrested. Caught just over the English border fleeing Scotland. Suppose she thought her cousin Elizabeth would forgive her treason. She is being held at Carlisle Castle." He took her hand. "The whole house is awake with the news, and I knew it would be the disruption needed."

The tears she'd fought so hard to contain fell, warm and silent, upon his shoulder. He held her for a long moment before helping her to her feet.

At last, he said, "No matter what, Beth, I was coming for you."

Beth gently pulled her hand away. "Go on. I'll catch up," she whispered, still trembling. "Let me compose myself before anyone sees me in such a state."

Gareth hesitated, his eyes still fixed on her.

"Please," she said softly.

He gave a slow nod. "Of course," he replied.

His smile at her was stiff, nothing like his usual smiles, though Beth did not hold this against him. She suspected she might not see one of Gareth's old smiles for a while yet, not until what had been done to his father was long past.

Alone, Beth made her way to the hearth and stood over Bayne's devices. Some she recognized as ordinary work tools. She found it difficult to imagine the wood saw and small hammer being used for nefarious purposes, but others made the bile rise in her throat. The pear-shaped globe with the metal rod. The miniature vice and corkscrew. All made her stomach curdle. Yet, the narrow-bladed knife with the serrated edge and bone handle caught her eye.

Warily, she looked toward the door, fearing Bayne appearing again at any moment. Hastily, she snatched the knife and slipped it into her apron pocket.

It wasn't wrong to rely on friends, but she must be able to defend herself. It was unwise to be defenseless in a world where men like Bayne roamed freely.

If Bayne wasn't done with her, then she wasn't finished with him, either.

As Beth had feared, her encounter with Bayne only deepened Gareth's rage. With Christmastide behind them, the queen's retinue had burrowed in to escape the worst of winter. Perhaps they would remain until spring. Beth had overheard Holbrook suggest as much to Lord Charles.

It was no time for revenge, no matter how fiercely she wished it for Gareth's sake. Danger no longer loomed at the manor gate. It walked the halls. It dined at their tables and pried into their lives with calculating eyes. Holbrook and Bayne passed silently through the corridors, lingered in doorways, and shadowed their days with ill intent. Now, the hidden priest hole—and the Sheffields' secret faith—teetered on the edge of discovery. One misstep, one ill-chosen word, and all could be lost.

But no matter how Beth tried, she could not subdue Gareth's wrath and convince him that punishing the queen's men now would only bring ruin upon them all. Nothing she said calmed him. Nothing quenched his fury.

Instead, Gareth sneaked away from his duties whenever he could, searching for Bayne or Holbrook, hoping to find them alone and unsuspecting, the newly whetted dagger on his belt always within reach.

Once, Beth found Gareth lurking outside the garderobe while Bayne relieved himself. Another time, as she replenished the candles, she glimpsed Gareth in the chapel shadows, watching as Holbrook knelt in prayer. Neither man realized how near they were to death. Until, finally, Beth had no choice but to seek Lady Eleanore's counsel.

"Since you cannot convince him otherwise," Eleanore said, her voice tight, "Gareth must return to the stable. The temptation for him to act is too great within these walls." Her eyes flicked about as if the plaster and timber were closing in on her, too.

The order came swiftly. That afternoon, Gareth said nothing as he packed his few belongings from the library. Yet, his eyes found Beth across the room, and she spun away, busying herself with the broom.

Parting the heavy curtain, Beth watched Gareth from the library window as he crossed the courtyard, head down against the bitter wind and back to the cold, hard barns, and she wondered if she had done what was best.

A day later, Beth was as deep in thought as the sawdust she swept when John startled her from behind.

"I hear Gareth left us," he said, glancing at the empty bed pallet. "Returned to the stables."

Beth nodded, unable to stop the welling of tears.

"It is my doing," she said, her voice trembling. "He was determined to avenge his father. Reckless and stubborn. Blind to everything around him."

John reached for Beth's arm, giving it a gentle squeeze. "You did what was right," he said softly. "As hard as that may seem."

"I hardly know right from wrong anymore. The realm sanctions torture. Murderers walk freely. My lord and lady defy the queen. And Gareth and I . . ." Her voice faltered. "We protect *heretics*!"

The word caught in her throat, but it was too late to take back.

John turned away.

"I'm sorry. Forgive me," she blurted. "I didn't mean that. You and Nicholas are my friends—*dear* friends—I'm only . . . confused." She pressed a hand to her forehead. "Gareth is my friend, too. But I fear I've betrayed him."

John turned back to her, his eyes steady and full of conviction. "Or saved him from his own folly and protected many others as well," he said. "Your head may be full of doubt, Beth, but your heart is in the right place. And decisions of the heart are sometimes the hardest of all."

<hr />

Beth had scarcely finished her midday meal when Kat slipped onto the bench across from her in the servants' kitchen, a tankard of ale, wedge of cheese, and a chunk of bread in her hands.

"Gareth's back at the stable," Kat said lightly, tearing off a piece of bread. "Pleases me well enough. I can see him regular again." She took a sip of ale, her eyes gleaming like a barn cat as she chewed and swallowed. "I think he missed my visits."

Beth set down her empty spoon, the taste of stew turning sour on her tongue. "Who told you he was back?" she asked.

Kat paused and then said, "Thomas. He's pleased about it, too."

Beth frowned. "Why would Thomas care?"

Kat leaned back, nimbly stretching her arms up into the air. "All the servants care, manor and stable alike." She took a long draught of ale then placed it on the table, her eyes never leaving Beth's. "The lord and lady are partial to you and Gareth. Everyone sees it. The easy errands. Warm beds. Wine sipped in a private chamber. You're favored, Beth. Everyone notices." Her gaze sharpened as she leaned forward. "And everyone talks, Beth—especially when favored servants take a fall."

Beth glanced around the kitchen, suddenly feeling the weight of the other servants' gazes upon her, calculating and cold. Eyes darted about. The swish of a broom, the steady rhythm of butter at the churn, the thump of boots carrying in wood—every move, every sound swirled around her. Faces she'd trusted turned away too quickly.

Beth remained silent as Kat walked off and stared into her empty bowl, her stomach suddenly sour. The warmth of the kitchen, the hum of the servants, the clatter of dishes—all of it felt different. It wasn't just Bayne or Holbrook that posed a danger. It was the sidelong glances of fellow servants who shared her bread; their eyes lowered in the halls.

How easily envy ignited—like a spark on dry hay.

13

GARETH

G areth opened the door to his childhood home, a door he had passed through countless times before, forever changed without his father.

He stood motionless at the threshold. For a long moment, his arrival went unnoticed, and he took in the memories of the small but loving space. The worn trestle table and bench, so humble. The drying herbs dangling from the rafters. The stool that stood by the hearth where his father once warmed himself after a long day's work. The peg by the door empty of the usual cloak and cap.

Dutifully, his mother, Agnes, fed another log into the fire under the hanging iron pot. The flame crackled, casting flickers of warmth across the dim cottage walls, but the chill lingered. Outside the door, the wood box sat only half full. Another quiet reminder that winter was upon them and his father was gone.

Gareth took the measure of his mother. The wrinkles around her eyes and lips had deepened even in such a short time, and her stature, once sure and straight, was now stooped.

When she finally turned and saw him, her head dropped, and she covered her face with her hands and wept.

Gareth crossed the room with a few quick strides and gathered her in his arms as she had done for him countless times when he was a boy. Silently, they stood together.

Then, all at once, the door burst open, and Rafe entered, struggling slightly with a bucket sloshing with water. His mother hastily wiped her eyes and pulled away, snatching up a torn shirt needing repair.

At the sight of Gareth, Rafe stopped short. The bucket slipped from his hands with a thud, water splashing over the threshold. Without a word, he ran to his brother and flung his arms around Gareth's waist, sobbing.

Gareth let him cling there for a long while, resting a gentle hand on the boy's head. His eyes brimmed as Rafe's small body shook like a fragile sparrow, and together they clung to each other in brotherly grief.

All the stubborn arguments with his father, all the pride and sharp words, fell away. Stripped bare, Gareth saw only the truth that his father only wanted what was best for him, a sternness rooted in steadfast love.

At last, he eased Rafe back and met his tear-streaked face. "Come now," he said softly. "Mother needs us to be strong. To carry on as a family."

Agnes looked up from her mending, blinking back tears. "You're staying?"

He nodded. "I mean to speak to Lord Sheffield. Go back and explain that I am needed here, given the circumstances. He'll understand, I hope," he said. He turned back to Rafe. "We'll look in on the smithy together. See what needs to be done."

Rafe's head bobbed eagerly, hope flickering in his reddened eyes.

"As much as we need the money," his mother said firmly, "there'll be no more poaching. Between the smithy and my mending, we'll make do."

"Won't you teach me to steal fish?" Rafe piped up, his voice lifting with curiosity.

Gareth shook his head. "No, Rafe. Mother is right. There'll be no more stealing." He shifted with unease. "I still have some money," he told his mother. "Enough to get us through for now, anyway."

"Not the money saved for leaving," his mother said quickly. "I won't have it."

"No, it's not that," he began, but she pressed on without hearing him.

"You must leave, Gareth, once we're on our feet. It's what you want. It's what you've always wanted," she said, her eyes widening. "Take on life as you've dreamt it. Be the farmer or the traveler you've always spoken of." She gestured to the modest room. "You're meant for more than this. Perhaps build your own smithy far from this place. We'll manage," she said, her voice breaking.

Gareth took her hands. "Or stay, and take on this one," he said. "Perhaps what I've always wanted was before me all along."

"Well," she murmured, brushing away tears. "You'll do as you will. You've always had a mind of your own . . . much like your father," she mused with a small sad smile. "And what of the girl?" his mother asked with knowing eyes.

Gareth's expression hardened. "Beth?"

She nodded. "Yes, the maidservant. She'll miss you, won't she? Rafe's told me about the way you look at her and the way it makes her blush. Your father and I found strength in each other. We built a life in that strength. Perhaps you can, too."

"That same girl betrayed me!" Gareth shot back bitterly. "Kept me from avenging Father's death!"

"And what would that have brought you?" his mother snapped, threading the needle with quick fingers. "A murderer's death!" She bit the thread and pulled it taut. "Doesn't sound like a betrayal to me."

Gareth fell silent, his thoughts a jumble of anger and regret. Perhaps he had judged Beth too harshly. Yet there was no time for that now. His course was set. He was going home.

He watched his mother fold the mended shirt and placed in the basket, her devotion to her family as steadfast as ever. "I can only pray someday to find a love like yours and Father's," he said finally.

His mother stared back, her voice low and steady. "Haven't you?"

The smithy stood quiet beneath a veil of soot and silence. Gareth and Rafe said nothing as they stepped inside, breathing in the stagnant air. Each felt the absence of the man who had once filled the space with the clang of iron and the deep timbre of his voice.

"There's much to be done, Rafe," Gareth said at last, handing the boy a cinder rake and bucket. "Clear out the coal ash from the fire bed. I'll relight the flame as soon as I return for good."

The forge had been cold for many days. The bricks sat lifeless, and the bellows sagged, deflated, like a lung no longer breathing—silenced like the breath of their father.

Gareth shoved the grief down deep. There wasn't time for mourning. The anvil needed scraping and oiling. Fresh coal would have to be hauled in before dusk. There was too much to do and only a short time left. Tomorrow, he'd return to Bodsworth one last time.

Outside, Gareth emptied the ash buckets behind the shed, shaking out the remnants of old fires.

"Good day to you, sir," came a voice behind him.

He turned sharply, heart pounding. Blood pulsed in his veins. "The shop is closed for now," he said, voice stiff. "I'll be taking things over . . . for my father. He's no longer here." His words caught, and he looked away, swallowing hard.

But the man remained.

He stepped forward and stuck out his hand. He was around his father's age, perhaps a little older, with broad shoulders and calloused hands marked by labor. His worn cap barely covered his wiry gray hair, but his eyes, deep-set and pale, held a kindness and a hint of sadness Gareth easily recognized. "My name is Peter. I'm sorry about your father. Word spread quickly."

Gareth nodded stiffly, unsure of what to say. He'd heard those words often in the past few days, but they still struck like a mallet to the chest. "Thank you," he said, glancing down at the ash that clung to his hands. "If you're here seeking work, I don't have money to pay for hired help."

Peter shook his head, his eyes never leaving Gareth's. "I work for Phelps, an olive oil merchant, taking orders and delivering barrels, although I know my way around a smith shop," he said, taking in the metal tools and forge. "That's not why I'm here." His voice lowered. "I'm looking for a man named John. He may be working as an apprentice carpenter for Nicholas Owens."

Gareth's legs nearly gave way. How did this man know John? He brushed the ash from his hands on his breeches and scooped up the bucket. "I know no such man," he said, turning to leave.

Peter reached for his arm. "Please—he is my son!" The desperate words landed like a blow, but Gareth continued walking, ignoring the deranged stranger, knowing the claim was false.

"I speak the truth!" Peter said, grasping at him again.

Gareth shrugged Peter's hand away. "But that's not the truth, sir! It's a lie!" Gareth replied angrily. "John is an orphan. Given over to the priory by his parents. Raised by monks."

The man's eyes brimmed with tears. "A tale spun to keep him safe," Peter said, his voice barely above a whisper.

Gareth turned to leave again, scolding himself silently for listening to the old fool.

"John is a priest," Peter burst out suddenly just before Gareth turned the corner.

Gareth halted mid-stride and put the bucket back down. He studied the man again. There was no trickery in his face, only weariness and something deeper. Pain. The kind that carved itself into the heart of a parent. Gareth recognized it—the same raw, aching look his own father had worn before the end. That desperate love.

Peter pressed on as Gareth listened intently. "John escaped the priory's destruction. He's been hiding as Nicholas Owen's apprentice—the man who builds priest holes." Peter locked eyes with Gareth. "I'll tell you everything."

Just then, the gravel crunched behind them. Both men turned. Rafe stood at the corner of the shed, eyes wide, lips parted.

"Not here," Gareth said, his voice firm. "Come with me."

Seated at a corner table at the alehouse, away from other patrons who gossiped as they ate their midday meal, Gareth took a long draught of ale.

"Does John know of you?" Gareth asked, setting down the tankard.

"No," Peter replied, staring into his mug. "He doesn't know me, and I don't know him. I delivered him safely to the priory when he was only a few hours old. But I've watched him from afar. Found out he'd been given over to Master Owen by the prior."

Gareth frowned. "And what of his mother?" he asked, as he shifted with unease.

"His mother?" Peter's eyes gleamed. "His mother," he said with a small smile, "was the grand lady of Abury Manor. Lady Sarah Barrell."

Gareth's mouth parted, but no words followed. Beth had told him Marge's story about a child born in shame. The baby whisked away by Lord Barrell. A story almost too strange to be believed.

They sat in silence for a long moment. The noise of the tavern filled the space between them—the scrape of benches, the indistinct murmur of laughter, the barkeep's voice rising at a spilled pitcher. But their corner stayed untouched by all of it, suspended from the surrounding reality.

Finally, Peter took a large swallow of ale and said, "I wasn't about to let that bastard murder my boy." His voice was low and tight. "That night, I rode out and intercepted the carriage on the road. Convinced Lord Barrell to let me do the deed. Said it was beneath the lord of the manor. That his secret was safe with me, Peter, his faithful servant." He let out a bitter laugh. "Me, the man who shared the lord's own bed with his wife . . . and who loved her dearly."

Gareth leaned closer. "Why tell me all this?" he asked. "Why now?"

Peter's jaw tightened. "Because John is in danger once more. Holbrook's and Bayne's priest hunting in the village is done, and it's by no accident that they've moved on to the manor."

Gareth nodded, his mind spinning. "The Lord and Lady Sheffield are under suspicion," he agreed. "The queen's men will pounce once they gather enough proof of their treason. I am sure of it. By God, we were careful. Damn careful." Gareth's empty tankard hit the table with a thud. Heads turned.

Peter raised a hand and scanned the room. "Careful is never enough. Tongues wag either for coin or under the lash. It's no secret the villagers want the priest hunters gone. What better way to send them off than to point them toward Bodsworth? Let the blood spill elsewhere."

Fear rose in Gareth's throat. "I've got to get back."

He went to stand, but Peter's hand shot across the table, pulling him back down. "There's one more thing," he said. "I brought a girl to the manor a while back. A girl named Beth. Hired to work in the scullery."

Gareth blinked. "You know Beth?"

"Beth Dudley, aye. Sarah loved that girl. Tried to make up for the wrongs done to her family."

Gareth's eyes widened at the news. "We're friends, Beth and I. Lady Eleanore pulled her from the kitchens to aid Master Owen's efforts."

Peter hesitated and then added, "She's in grave danger, too."

Gareth pushed to his feet again with a fresh urgency, and, this time, Peter stood with him.

"I'm going with you," Peter said. "The lord at Hinlip Hall in Worcestershire is a Catholic sympathizer. Nicholas built priest holes there, too."

"Will they be safe?" Gareth asked, his words thick with worry.

Peter looked him straight in the eye, his voice grim. "Is there ever such a thing?"

14

BETH

Beth crossed the frost-hardened courtyard, clutching her shawl tighter against the biting January wind. The other hand gripped a tin bucket of kitchen scraps meant for Fritz.

She had not spoken to Gareth in over a week, not since his dismissal from the manor. A foolish hope convinced her that a kind gesture toward Fritz would grant her a sliver of forgiveness.

"He's not here," a voice from behind said as she approached Gareth's bed pallet near the saddle benches.

She turned sharply and saw Thomas leaning against a stall, a pitchfork in hand. His gaze was hard and suspicious.

"Where is he?" she asked, trying to keep her tone light.

Thomas's eyes narrowed slightly. She did not know the lad well, only what Gareth had told her: stories full of brazen antics and foolery, jokes and tales between friends shared over tankards. He'd spoken of Thomas as a trusted pal.

Thomas didn't answer at once, then said in a guarded tone, "Gone to Surrey to see his family. Telford gave him leave. Thought it best. That's all I know. Mostly keeps to himself these days since his father . . ."

A pang of guilt lit through her, and she shifted the bucket in her grip. "I only came to feed Fritz. Nothing more."

Thomas's gaze moved to the bucket, then back to her. "He's a barn dog. Stable boys feed him."

He was right, perhaps, but only partly. The stable boys might have shared their scraps with Fritz, but the little dog always waited for Gareth's hand, was always at his heel like a shadow. The dog loved company as much as scraps, but it was Gareth's companionship he sought.

Silence stretched between them. Beth felt the frost, not only in the frigid air, but in Thomas's stance and the heaviness of his eyes on her. Kat had spoken true. Something had shifted not just with the manor servants but here in the barn, too. It was everywhere. The feeling wafted around her like an ill-begotten mist.

"I'll leave the bucket, then," she murmured, and moved to set it by the pallet.

"And I'll see Fritz gets it," Thomas replied.

Beth paused at the door, the stiff wind tugging at her shawl. "Thank you."

Back in her chamber, Beth changed into a dry smock and wimple, hanging her damp clothes on a peg. She crossed to the small mirror above the washstand to tuck a few stray hairs under the white linen, but something caught her eye. She stepped back from the washstand, frowning. The bar of lye soap was in a different place. It now sat on the opposite side of the basin, not on top of the wash rag where she always left it.

Heart pounding, Beth hastily scanned the room and then rushed to the trunk. She flung open the lid and reached behind the loose piece of lining. The crucifix pendant was gone. The floor seemed to tilt beneath her. Her thoughts tumbled, but only one name came to her lips.

Beth hastily tied her apron and hurried down the corridor to the chamber they'd once both shared. Not bothering to knock, Beth pushed open the door. Kat lay curled up on her mattress, back to the door, as if asleep.

"Where is it?" Beth snapped, her voice sharp with fury. "I know you have the pendant!"

Kat didn't move.

"I'm tired of your games! Give it back!"

The silence that followed was strange—wrong.

Beth's anger faltered. "Kat?" she asked, softer now. "Are you ill?"

Gently, Beth eased down on the coverlet beside her. Kat stirred and then slowly turned over.

Beth gasped. A dark bruise bloomed beneath her eye, swollen and raw.

"My God, what happened?" she whispered. "Who did this to you?"

Kat's lip trembled as she reached for Beth, her eyes wide with a look of terror. "Bayne," she choked out, crumbling against Beth, sobbing. "It was Bayne. He found me alone in the henhouse this morning. He pushed me down into the hay . . . forced me, Beth! He forced me!"

Beth stiffened at her words. "Hush, now," she murmured, her voice low and steady as though she were soothing a babe. "You're safe now. All will be well."

Kat pulled back, wild-eyed. "I dropped the basket," she cried. "The eggs are all broken, Beth! They're ruined!"

Beth blinked, startled by the sudden shift. "It doesn't matter," she said gently.

Kat clutched her arms with a desperate grip. "Don't you understand? They're all broken!" she repeated, her voice rising. "Annie will be furious. She'll tell her ladyship. No one will believe me. They'll say I'm lying to cover my clumsiness."

Beth swallowed hard, her heart aching as Kat's world unraveled before her. She eased the poor girl back down onto the bed. "I'm here now, Kat, and I'll help you. You're not alone."

Beth helped the poor girl wash and gave her warm broth, wishing for something stronger. She sat with her until the shaking calmed and her breath steadied. Kat seemed only slightly better by the time Beth eased her back into bed. As Beth turned to go, Kat reached out and grasped her hand, her eyes still wide and glassy. "Put it back together in the morning," she murmured. "I'll make it right again ..."

Beth gave her a gentle squeeze, but the words still chilled her. She slipped out of the room and hurried down to the kitchen.

Annie sat at a long table, quill in hand, reviewing the day's receipts.

"What is it?" she asked the moment she saw Beth's face, putting down the parchments. "You're as pale as bleached linen!"

Beth sank onto the bench beside her and discreetly told her everything—Kat, the henhouse, Bayne.

"I fear for her," Beth finished, her voice trembling. "She's not in her right mind!"

Annie's face darkened. "I don't doubt what Bayne did—the heathen!" she seethed, slamming her hand against the table. "I'll go up to her. See for myself. Might be best to send for the herbalist, too." She shook her head slowly, sorrow in her eyes. "She was hard on you, I know. Sharp-tongued and strange in her ways. But it's often the hard ones that break the easiest inside."

Beth nodded and was about to ask what else could be done when a guard entered the kitchen and approached them

"Come with me," he said to Beth, his tunic bearing the Tudor rose over the heavy mesh of his armor. "Reverend Holbrook's orders."

Frozen rain pelted the library windows, blurring the early morning view into a tapestry of gray and white. Beth kept her head low, lifting her eyes only enough to take stock of the others.

Lady and Lord Sheffield sat opposite her at the long library table, their hands folded, thin smiles nervously pinned to their faces.

At the head of the table, Reverend Holbrook leafed through one of several books stacked before him, his fingers turning the pages with delicate care. The soft rustle of parchment and the crackle of the fire were the only sounds, except for the scuff of boots produced by Bayne, who paced the length of the bookshelves like a baited bear, hands clasped behind him, awaiting his master's signal.

Beth watched him with growing unease, keenly aware of the truth neither man knew. Behind the paneled wall in the priest hole, two souls hid in the dark, cramped space meant only for one. A small chair provided room to sit and perhaps sleep on the floor in a curled position. The space was meant to hide someone for a short time, not days.

How long would they last?

They had been up all night with most of the attention fixed on Lord and Lady Sheffield, beckoned to the library under the guise of questioning over the disappearance of John and Nicholas, but the hours had dragged on over endless tedious examination. But then, the tone shifted. This was no inquiry—it was detainment.

Holbrook finally spoke, his voice cutting through the silence. "Lord Charles," he said, his eyes flicking up from the page. "Do you not attend Sunday services in the manor chapel?"

Charles met his gaze evenly. "On occasion. Whenever duty allows, yes," he answered, staring steadfastly at the cleric. "When it does not, I pay the tax to the realm for any absences, as is required by law."

"And your wife?" Holbrook turned the page. "She abstains sometimes as well?"

"You are mistaken, my lord," Lady Eleanore answered quickly, her tone firm. "I attend services."

Holbrook tapped a gnarled finger against the page before him, counting under his breath.

"Not so, my good lady," he said. "You have missed several services. I have it recorded right here." He tapped the ledger with the quill. "And no tax paid."

"Recorded by whom!" Charles snapped, the rigid edge of temper rising in his voice. "Are there spies in my household?"

Bayne halted, pivoting sharply. "There are no spies! Only loyal subjects to Her Majesty!" he growled.

Holbrook raised a hand to calm him, and Bayne turned back to the bookshelves.

Lord Charles held the cleric's gaze. "Are the queen's subjects not English before they are Catholic or Protestant?" he asked pointedly.

Holbrook's smiled showed no warmth. His eyes were piercing and cold. "Her subjects are whatever she declares them to be." He snapped shut the ledger. "If they are heretics? They burn. Traitors? They burn. And if they are priests?" He turned to Bayne. "The fire is twice as hot. English queens always bring fire for priests. Do they not?"

Bayne's boots creaked on the newly laid floor as he turned from the shelves. "And precious little water to quench it," he added, his lips twisting into a cruel grin.

Beth's stomach lurched with disgust, bile rising in her throat, but she held fast to her composure.

"And now we come to you, Beth, the new scullery maid of the manor." He glanced down at a random scrap of paper. "Promoted, I see, to a special envoy to Lady Eleanore."

"She reads, writes, and comports herself far beyond a kitchen maid," Eleanore cut in vehemently.

"Is that so?" The reverend leaned in with mock curiosity. "Does that refined conduct also include harboring heresy? Defying Her Majesty's penal code?"

"The girl is no heretic!" Lord Charles snapped, his voice clipped but steady.

Bayne strode to the table and brought his fist down onto it with a smack that made Beth flinch. He opened his hand, and a silver crucifix pendant glinted in his palm. "Then she is a thief!"

Beth's throat tightened, and a wave of nausea churned in her stomach once again. "I am neither," she choked. "I found the cross on the ground during an errand in the village."

Reverend Holbrook began scribbling with his quill, scratching the dry parchment in long, determined strokes. "And you didn't endeavor to find its owner? Report the discovery to Lord Charles?"

Beth thought hard. "I believed the metal was worth something. Worth more than the idolatry it represents. I meant to sell it. It was foolish. I understand that now."

". . . and dangerous," Holbrook added, still writing.

"She is merely guilty of greed," Lord Charles said. "Nothing more."

"Perhaps," Holbrook conceded. "We are finished for the day and will reconvene on the morrow." He turned to Lady Eleanore. "Sir Bayne and I will take our evening meal in the parlor."

The men left, the heavy door thudding shut behind them. Beth sprang to her feet and rushed to the bookcase, reaching to open the false panel.

"Wait," Lord Charles told her and hurried to the door. He pressed his ear against the wood, listening until the echo of boot steps faded down the corridor. Then he nodded.

Beth pulled open the false panel. It teetered backwards on its hinges, revealing the hollow space behind it.

John and Nicholas scurried out onto the floor, Nicholas moaning in pain.

"Bring water," Charles said. Eleanore hurried to the sideboard, grabbing the pitcher and a cup.

Beth knelt beside Nicholas. "What is it? What pains you?"

"My back, child," he whispered, wincing. "The hours in that wretched hole have done me in."

"I'll fetch a liniment," Beth said, rising to her feet.

John stood above them, rubbing his arms briskly. "We crouched in the dark for what felt like an eternity."

"It was an eternity," Lord Charles replied grimly. "Hours of detention meant to break us down. If they don't know you're here, John, they're dangerously close. Neither of you is safe in these apartments any longer. Tonight, you'll hide in the wine cellar. It's the only place left unsearched—for now. We'll find a way out for you both, but until then, you must vanish from sight."

"I'm frightened," Lady Eleanore said suddenly, placing a hand on her chest.

"As am I," her husband answered swiftly, turning to her with eyes dark and serious. "We stand to lose everything, my love—even our lives."

John cocked his head at Charles. "Had you not weighed the consequences of the undertaking from the start?" he asked.

Charles looked away, not answering.

Lady Eleanore stared at Beth, an eyebrow arched. "Why on God's earth did you have that crucifix?"

Beth hesitated. "A stranger dropped it outside the carriage while I was visiting Mistress Marge," she replied carefully.

Lord Charles sighed, pinching the bridge of his nose. "It was foolish to bring it back here, Beth. We're all under such scrutiny." His voice was weary, and the lines around his eyes had deepened over the past few days.

He glanced at the closed door and then back at her. "And to think I hoped they believe you to be only a common thief and not a heretic. God help us. What have we become?"

15

GARETH

Gareth rode beside Peter as he pulled the wagon to a halt, finally reaching the manor stable. It was mid-afternoon, the height of the day for stable chores, but an unusual stillness hung in the air.

Gareth swung down from the bench seat, securing the reins to a hitching post, and Peter followed him inside the stable. The cool air was strangely quiet. The scent of sweat and hay lingered, but the usual banter among the stable lads was gone.

Gareth spotted Barnaby, one of the younger lads, lugging a feed bucket, and caught him by the arm. "What's happened? Why is the lord's horse not saddled and ready?"

Barnaby, a gap-toothed lad in a stained wool cloak, glanced around warily before answering. "His lordship won't be riding today. Word is he and the lady are under suspicion. They say heresy—maybe even hiding priests," he whispered before stumbling along.

The flush drained from Gareth's face, and Peter grabbed his arm. "We must move fast! Make a plan!"

"Not here," Gareth said sharply, eyes scanning the barn.

Keeping their heads down, they made their way toward the servants' kitchen. To avoid attention, Gareth grabbed a handful of logs from the woodpile, and Peter hoisted a small barrel of oil from the wagon.

The kitchen, usually alive with the clatter of dishes and chatter of servants taking a meal between chores, was eerily somber. The hearth crackled, but there was no laughter, no shouting of orders. Conversation was kept to whispers.

Gareth dumped the logs into the woodbox beside the hearth and nodded for Peter to set the oil on the table. His eyes caught Annie speaking in hushed tones with a steward. The steward shook his head grimly and walked away.

Peter hung back while Gareth approached the cook. Her eyes were red from crying, and seeing Gareth brought a fresh bout of tears.

"Hell is raining down on us, I hear," he murmured, pulling her into a brief embrace.

Annie clung to him for a heartbeat, then pulled away. "Worse," she said, her voice breaking. She glanced around and leaned closer. "It's Kat. She's not well. Bayne found her collecting eggs. Beat her and—forced her." She looked away.

Gareth clenched his jaw, but Annie wasn't finished.

"The queen's men have the lord and lady," she whispered. "They're questioning Beth, too."

Gareth's eyes flashed. "Where is she?"

"In the library, last I knew. But the questioning ended an hour ago. She's likely returned to her chamber by now."

Without a word, Gareth turned and motioned for Peter to follow. They crossed swiftly through the pantry into the great hall, heading to the grand staircase.

Behind him, Annie's voice called out a warning. "Careful, lad! You're no longer allowed in the private apartments! In case you've forgotten!"

But Gareth had not forgotten. Beth's actions had brought him back to the stables. But it was his own pride, his own foolishness, that had made him blame her for it. She was only trying to protect him—to protect them all.

He would make things right but, for now, he must see her safe.

They climbed the wide stone stairs two steps at a time and paused at the top. The corridor was quiet except for a few servants tending their daily duties.

Gareth led the way to Lady Eleanore's hallway, stopping at Beth's bedchamber. He knocked lightly, then entered with Peter close behind.

Beth sat near the window on a small stool, her figure still and silhouetted in the soft afternoon light. She looked like a beautiful caged bird, staring out at a cruel, unforgiving world.

Gareth took a few steps forward. At the sound of movement, she turned, her eyes landing on Peter. In an instant, she rushed from the window.

"Peter! Do my eyes deceive me? What are you doing here?" she cried, throwing her arms around him in a firm embrace.

"The tale is long, my girl," he answered, his eyes twinkling with a familiar fondness.

Peter cleared his throat and cast a look at Gareth—a silent message passing between them.

"I'll take my leave for a moment," Gareth said, stepping back to give them space. "I'd like to check on Kat."

Beth nodded solemnly. "I tried to comfort her as best I could, but she's in a bad way."

"I know of former nuns living secular lives now. They'll take her in. Help her," Peter said. "John and I can take her there."

"John?" Beth's brows furrowed. "How do you know John?"

Gareth moved to the door. "Best I leave you to it, Peter," he said and slipped out, closing the door behind him.

A short time later, Gareth sat beside Kat, still curled in her bed, wrapped tightly in the coverlet. She moaned softly. A mug of broth sat untouched on the side table, long gone cold.

"Kat? It's me, Gareth," he said, keeping his voice calm.

Slowly, her fingers drew back the edge of the blanket. She turned toward him, her blank eyes searching his face as if assembling a memory from fragments. "My friend," she murmured.

Gareth pulled the stool closer. "Yes, Kat, I am your friend . . . always."

Her face twisted, clouded by sudden uncertainty. "Am I home? Where's Mother? Tell her I'm sorry about the eggs. It couldn't be helped." She searched his face with terror-stricken eyes. "You'll keep the whip away from her, won't you?"

Gareth reached for her hand to comfort her, but she shirked away from his touch.

"There's a place you could go," he said softly, unsure if she understood. "They'll be kind to you. Take care of you. Help you recover your strength. But you have to trust me. Do you trust me, Kat?"

Kat gave a faint smile, distant and unfocused, then turned away, retreating back into the shadows.

16

BETH

Two small rush candles were the only light in Blackthorne's stall, their soft flicker casting shadows across the beams. Beth stroked its neck as the horse tugged mouthfuls of hay from the bale.

"Eat well, boy," Beth said. "You've a long road ahead."

Gareth emerged from the tack room with a saddle, his face unreadable in the half-light. He slung the saddle across Blackthorne's back and reached for the girth strap hanging below. The gelding snorted and side-stepped at the sudden cinch as Gareth gave the strap a firm tug.

"Easy! You'll hurt him," Beth scolded.

Gareth didn't look up. "Blackthorne's well accustomed to it," he said, giving the strap one last tug. "And I know just how hard to pull. You wouldn't want the saddle slipping on the road, would you?" Gareth glanced at her, studying her face. "All will be well, Beth. We all must do our duty, and I'll be back as soon as I can." He offered her a half-smile.

But Beth didn't smile back. As much as she loved her friends and wanted them safely delivered from danger, she didn't care for Gareth's part in the Sheffield's plan to help Nicholas and John escape. It was fraught with danger and hastily thought out. The fear that, once again, Gareth was in harm's way coursed through her like ice. "A guard could escort Nicholas to Worcestershire. Why must it be you?"

He crossed to a peg and pulled down the bridle. "The manor guards can no longer be trusted."

"What about Martin, the carriage driver? He was loyal enough when I rode with him to Surrey."

Gareth shook his head. "Lord Charles chose me. I'll take Nicholas to Lord Habington to continue his work. That's the plan. And Peter will get John on a ship to Spain once Kat's settled. It's the only place he'll be safe now."

"Buy why you?" she pressed. "There are others. Why must it be you?"

His hands stilled on the bridle. "Because I know the roads. I know how to vanish when danger is near. And I won't fail them, Beth. I won't let anyone else fall to Bayne's cruelty."

Beth stared at the hay strewn floor, blinking fast. "And what of you? What if you don't come back?"

He stepped closer, brushing the straw from her sleeve. "Then you'll carry on. Like always," he told her, hesitating. "Beth . . . I've wronged you."

The words surprised her, and she met his gaze.

"When you spoke to Lady Eleanore . . . I know now you were only trying to save me from myself. From my rage. Not betray me."

A silence stretched between them, heavy with the things neither dared say aloud.

Beth looked away, her throat tightening. "If Holbrook and Bayne had never found the crucifix, they might've been well on their way by now. Off to terrorize another village. Hold hostage another manor." She paused, choking on the words. "And violate another servant girl!" Her hands flew to her face as the heaving sobs rose from within.

The bridle slipped from his hand. He crossed the space between them and gathered her in his arms. She didn't resist. Her guilt and sadness poured out against him.

"Listen," he said gently, pressing his hands to her face, forcing her to look at him. "You couldn't have stopped any of this. You hear me?"

Her breath hitched as she tried to believe him.

"The Sheffields were careless," he continued. "Have been for a long time. That's the truth of it. Flaunting their absence from Sunday service. Avoiding the fines. Latin prayers whispered behind closed doors. The blame does not lie with you."

Beth shook her head weakly. "But I—"

"No," he said firmly. "They brought this plague on themselves."

She stared at him, eyes red and glistening. Slowly, she nodded just as his lips met hers. The kiss was warm and tender and filled with everything they had kept secret in their hearts. The struggles of the world fell away, and she wanted nothing more than to stay in that moment forever.

Finally, Beth laid her head on his chest, unwilling to move. "Come back to me, Gareth Montgomery. Or I'll never forgive you."

Later that night, after life at the manor had quieted into slumber, Beth helped Kat rise from her bed as if leading a child. The girl remained silent, her eyes a vacant gaze, as Beth gathered her meager belongings, pushing them down into a satchel.

A wool shawl, apron, smock and a few undergarments were all she had in the world. Beth wrapped the shawl around her shoulders and then slipped her arms into another heavy cloak Lady Eleanore had discreetly provided. It dwarfed her frame, but warmth mattered more than fit.

Beth didn't know how long the journey would take to the former nuns Peter had spoken of. The women had suffered their own hardships, and Beth could only hope they would help Kat and offer solace, but the journey would be long and cold. Bitterly so. Of that, Beth was sure.

Remembering the bread carefully wrapped on the side table, she slipped the loaf into the satchel that Annie insisted she take, as Marge had done for her on a day long past.

Kat had not cried since the night before. The silence was heavier than the tears. The girl was a fragile shell. There was no malice left in her now. Remembering the petty games and cutting words left no anger in Beth's heart, only a sad ache.

"Come," Beth said gently, placing a steadying hand on her back. "Let's get you some place safe."

Beth led Kat down the servants' staircase, and she wondered if Kat knew this would be her last time within the manor walls. Perhaps it was better if she didn't. The air grew colder as they made their way down the lower corridor. Footsteps echoed faintly from somewhere far away, most likely a hall boy feeding the many fires. Beth pressed on, guiding Kat past storerooms and stacked barrels.

As they approached the end of the hall, the sound of muffled voices drifted from the buttery. Beth stopped abruptly and pulled Kat aside into a dark recess behind a pillar. The girl sagged into the shadows, too dazed to question it.

"You're sure," came Bayne's voice, low and sharp.

Beth swallowed. Why was Bayne in the servants' quarters? She leaned in, her heart pulsing hard against her chest.

"Yes, sir," came Thomas's voice—clear and certain. "The men have been hiding here at the manor house. One is a carpenter. The other's a *priest!*"

Beth's hand flew to her mouth.

Bayne gave a low, knowing grunt. "A priest, aye. How do you know?"

"I laid a trap," Thomas replied, sounding pleased with himself. "Decorated one of the lord's prized palfreys for Saint Stephen's Day during Christmastide. Turned out to be the right bait. It brought the servant girl, Beth, and the carpenter, Master Owen, running. The priest, too, the quiet one, John." He paused, unable to contain his smugness.

"Later," he continued, "I caught John offering a blessing. Gave it to Gareth Montgomery as he left the stables. A priest's cowl and all. Been parading as Owen's apprentice this whole time."

Bayne let out a long, slow whistle, like a huntsman rousing the hounds. "Where have Owen and his *apprentice* disappeared to?"

Thomas hesitated. "I don't know."

"Still, you've done well," Bayne said. "Perhaps the lord and lady need more persuading. They may know where their guests have gone."

The jingle of coins being passed ended the conversation. The two men left the buttery; the shuffle of their boots became distant down the hall.

Beth waited until there was silence. Beside her, Kat shivered, unaware of the words that threatened them all. She squeezed her eyes shut for a moment, then opened them. She had to get Kat out and warn the others.

Beth rushed through the kitchen gardens, her fingers clenched tightly around Kat's hand, as they made their way past the frost-covered herbs, gravel crunching under their quick steps. Up ahead, Beth saw the flicker of torches at the cowshed tucked behind the larger knot garden, away from sight, where they were all to meet.

Her chest ached at the thought of what she had to tell Gareth. Thomas's betrayal would cut deep. The thought that such a friendship had been tossed aside for a few coins, breaking a loyalty forever, saddened her. For what? A man like Bayne?

When they reached the shed, the smell of dung and rotting timber greeted them. Peter and John sat ready in the wagon, cloaked against the cold. Father and son—finally together. It was a bittersweet reunion carved by fate.

It was Peter's idea to travel under the guise of merchants, and she hoped the ruse would hold under scrutiny. Oil barrels still loaded the wagon, and tucked within a few empty casks, John hid his priestly vestments, communion linen, a well-wrapped chalice, and other precious items.

She turned to Kat, whose pale face peered up at her from beneath the bulky hood. "It's time," Beth said gently and helped her up the wagon step.

The men reached down and pulled her up, nestling her between them, and Beth thought she saw Kat look down at her and offer a grateful smile.

She nodded back with a smile of her own. In her heart, she wished Kat well, sending her a silent prayer.

Peter looked down from the wagon seat. "Looks like this is farewell again," he said to her with a tight voice.

Tears welled in Beth's eyes. She reached up, her fingers latching onto the coarse fabric of his trouser leg. "I have to know," she said softly. "Was it you who left the crucifix that evening in Surrey? The stranger in the shadows?"

His lips curled into a wry smile. "Aye, I meant to give you the cross. Tell you who I was. Ask you to pass it along to John. But I could never get you away from that damn driver, and I ended up dropping it trying to get away."

"Martin . . ." Beth let out a soft, breathy laugh. "He is a man of duty, no doubt."

Peter chuckled faintly.

Her tone turned serious again. "Bayne has the pendant now. You'll never get it back."

"I don't need it," Peter said, glancing at John. "I have something far more precious than a silver cross."

John gave his father's arm a pat. "As have I," he said.

Beth turned to the group. Her gaze found Gareth and lingered there. "It was Thomas," she said quietly. "He decorated the horses on Saint Stephen's Day. Saw us scramble to hide it. It was a trap. And he witnessed John giving you a blessing. He told Bayne everything . . . and was paid for it."

"That bastard," Gareth muttered under his breath.

Beth stepped closer, her tone softening. "I'm sorry, Gareth. He was your friend."

Gareth's jaw clenched. "No more," he answered, turning away.

Peter looked down at them. "We're all in grave danger," he said. "If Bayne finds out our plans, he'll be on our scent in no time. We best be off." He turned to Gareth and Nicholas. "You as well. I'll try to send word once we're safe."

A tear slipped down Beth's cheek as she clutched the folds of her cloak.

"God bless all of you," John called as Peter gave the reins a flick.

The wagon jerked forward with the creak of wood and the jangle of harness as Nicholas and Gareth stepped beside her. Together, they watched the wagon rattle down the path and disappear into the night, away from the priest hunters, toward uncertain refuge.

Gareth turned to Nicholas. "Let's go," he said. "There are only a few hours left before dawn breaks."

Nicholas nodded, his expression solemn. He hefted his satchel and worn leather pouch onto his back, wincing at the weight. The pouch held all the precious drafts—his life's work in scroll and sketch, the code to secret hiding places yet to be built.

Gareth climbed into the saddle and then reached down, helping Nicholas swing up behind him.

"Get away from here as soon as you can," Gareth told Beth. "Head to Surrey. To my mother's place. I'll meet you there."

Gareth looked down at her, and their eyes locked. Her steady stare held the same warning she had given him in the barn. *Come back to me.*

17

BETH

Hours later, dawn broke, rousing the manor from its uneasy slumber. Beth stayed in the shadows, finding a sack of grain in the storeroom to rest on. She uncurled and rose from the cold flagstone floor. Her back and neck protested as she stretched.

Above her, the manor house was waking. Boots thudded. Voices called out. The day had begun.

Gareth's words lingered in her mind. *Get to Surrey. To my mother.* He was right, and she would, but first she must warn Lady Eleanore of Thomas's treachery. She had to catch her mistress in her bedchamber alone. No one was to be trusted now. Bayne's spies were everywhere.

Beth slipped from the storeroom and crept up the servants' staircase, pausing at every landing, listening for guards. Head bent low, she hurried to Eleanore's private apartments. As she reached her ladyship's bedchamber, she pressed her ear against the door. Hearing nothing, she knocked softly and then slipped inside.

Pale morning light filtered through the paned glass. The fireplace held the remains of smoldering embers; the blaze having long gone out.

Lady Eleanore sat at her dressing table, still in her bedclothes, her hair unbound and loose around her shoulders. A brush sat idly in her lap as she stared trance-like into the watery blur of the mirror.

"My lady?" Beth said softly.

Eleanore turned. Her eyes were distant. "Nicholas and John. Are they gone?" she asked before Beth could speak.

"Yes, my lady," Beth replied. "They departed in the early hours. John to the port of London—he sails for Spain. Nicholas to Hindlip Hall under Lord Habington's protection. Everything is as planned."

"And what of the servant girl?"

"She travels with John as well."

Eleanore studied her hands in her lap. "And you're certain the women will tend to her?"

"I was told they would take her in. She'll be well cared for," Beth replied.

"Very well. I will pray for her . . . what she must bear cannot be easy."

Beth blinked and brushed away the tear that slipped from her eye.

Eleanore looked up. "Godspeed to them all." She took a deep breath, exhaling slowly. "I will inform Lord Charles. It will bring some measure of comfort." She picked up the hairbrush from her lap and held it out to Beth. "Would you help me dress? Reverend Holbrook wishes to question the lord and me again after we break our fast." Then her head tilted slightly. "You must leave, Beth," she said, as if an afterthought. "Reverend Holbrook has little with to hold us. Unpaid taxes. That's all, really. The priest hole still remains hidden." Her eyes narrowed. "But you—having that crucifix—will be your downfall."

Beth shook her head. "That may be true. The hole may still be safe, but the cleric knows about John and Nicholas. Thomas, a stable lad, told Bayne," she said earnestly. "I heard it myself. That's why I'm here."

Eleanore inhaled sharply. "Then they'll demand confessions! Drag us to the tower." Her voice was barely a whisper. "Put us to the rack . . ."

"You are a noble," Beth said quickly, trying to calm her. "They would never."

But the blush on Eleanore's cheeks was gone, and Beth noticed her hands tremble as she helped her finish dressing.

"Now that you are warned, I will go, but first there are some favors I must ask," Beth said, her tone solemn.

Eleanore's eyebrows raised. "What is it?"

"Blackthorne . . . a stable horse. I want Gareth to have him."

Eleanore leaned back in her chair. "I cannot just give away one of my husband's prized palfreys," she said, waving her hand.

"Not a palfrey," Beth said. "A workhorse, one that Gareth has looked after since birth. Perhaps a final payment for all he has done."

Eleanore's brows furrowed for a moment, then she nodded. "Very well. What else?"

"My dowry," Beth said steadily, "I wish to give it to Marge, the cook who cared for me."

"But why?"

Tears welled in Beth's eyes once more. "Marge gave me everything when I had nothing. She was more of a mother to me than anyone, even Lady Sarah. It's time I gave something back."

Eleanore blinked in surprise. "But I thought you were leaving. The dowry was meant to offer you a good life, a stable one. How will you care for yourself?"

"The same way the rest of the peasants in the village do," Beth replied. "The same way I always have. By working."

Eleanore's voice softened. "Where am I to find this cook?"

"Martin, the driver who took me to Surrey—he'll know where to find her."

Unease crept into Beth's bones like winter's bite. The noose was closing in on the Sheffields.

Beth delayed her escape to Surrey, needing to be sure of the Sheffields' loyalty. Until now, they had been trustworthy. The lord and lady's cause rose above allegiance to the queen; they were steadfast in the conviction of their faith.

Yet, the terror in Lord Charles's eyes while being questioned by Holbrook had left Beth with a nagging feeling, and she wondered if the lord could truly be trusted.

The Sheffields and the queen's men broke their fast together in the great hall. Beth hid behind a stone pillar off to the side, away from prying eyes but close enough to listen.

After finishing their meal in uneasy silence, Bayne slid a ledger and quill toward Holbrook, who studied the documents with solemn care.

At length, Holbrook lifted his gaze, his eyes flicking to Eleanore, then to Charles. "Let us get straight to the matter," he said, placing his elbows on the table and tenting his long fingers together. "You have been harboring a priest and a heretic."

Eleanore's hand flew to her throat as Charles opened his mouth to speak.

Holbrook smiled faintly. "Let's have none of that," he told Charles. "There's no denying it. Sir Bayne is very good at what he does. He has served Her Majesty for many years. I trust his judgment completely."

"A servant who deals in torture and fear!" Charles shot back, his voice rising.

Unmoved, Holbrook tapped his chin in contemplation, his tone most thoughtful. "Treason is not a matter to be trifled with, even for nobles. Should the queen show mercy, you'd still be cast from her favor. The fines alone would be ruinous. You could not remain here, of course," he added, his eyes drifting over the fine tapestries and silver goblets. "You'd be left to beg for the charity of your kin." His eyes settled on Eleanore, her face blanched white. "Tell me. Do you have any such kin?"

Bayne chuckled darkly. "Things may become quite un-comfortable for you," he added, flexing his fingers through his leather glove, the threat in his tone promising far more than lost riches.

"Now, now, Sir Bayne, let's not get ahead of ourselves," Holbrook soothed, his eyes gleaming with delight.

From behind the pillar, ice coursed through Beth's veins as the cleric's noose drew tighter.

Holbrook turned to Charles. "Then again," he said smoothly, "if you possessed information that would be helpful to Her Majesty, perhaps in exchange for clemency . . . well, it might bode well for you. We know the priest and the carpenter—the clever builder of priest holes—are gone."

Charles cleared his throat. "What more information do you need?" he replied, clearly shaken.

Holbrooks's eyes narrowed. "Where did they go?"

"Charles, don't!" Eleanore's voice cut through the room, her eyes pleading with him.

"I will need what you promise in writing, of course," Charles said coldly, ignoring Eleanore.

"Of course," the cleric replied, waving his hand at Bayne. "Have the papers drawn."

Bayne nodded with a grunt.

"Very well," Charles said. "Nicholas is heading for Hindlip Hall, and John flees to London. He seeks refuge in Spain."

Eleanore gasped, turning to her husband in disbelief. "Why, Charles? After all we've done! After—everything!"

Charles remained silent, his eyes fixed on the far wall.

"You're a coward," she said, her voice trembling. "And a fool."

"We must make haste!" Bayne barked, spinning on his heel, but Holbrook raised a placating hand, stopping him, tempering his hound once more.

"Why?" the reverend murmured. "To what point? Let the heretic reach Hindlip. Let him settle in. Think himself safe." He sipped his wine, lips curling into a satisfied smile. "Then we'll pounce. The horses are ready. We'll leave by midday."

The floor beneath Beth blurred as she pressed her forehead against the cold pillar, steadying herself. There was no way to warn her friends. No way to protect them from the lord's betrayal. Lord Charles had given them up so easily—so callously. Holbrook's noose had closed, and the only souls who hung in the balance were her friends and Lady Eleanore.

Holbrook gathered his parchments and rose. "And now, you shall show us the priest hole."

Beth made her way to the kitchen. Powerless to send word to the others about Charles's deception, she knew what must be done. Her hand moved down to her hip, to the stolen knife, feeling the outline beneath her gown.

She hoped to catch Annie alone, but the poor woman stood near the pantry entrance with Master Hobbs, who prattled on about overcooked tarts.

The galley table overflowed with haunches of meat, bowls of puddings, and heaps of vegetables and herbs, awaiting the day's preparation.

For a heartbeat Beth lingered, remembering sitting with Kat cutting potatoes, flinching at the girl's hurtful barbs, and she realized the memory no longer stung.

Swiftly, she scooped up the scrap bucket and threw on a shawl hanging on the peg, covering her head and shoulders.

The wintry morning air hurt her lungs as she hurried to the stables. In the courtyard, the queen's retinue sat around a morning fire, warming themselves as they waited for orders. Their eyes followed the curve of Beth's hips, and one or two called out for her company, but head bent low, she ignored them and pressed on.

Inside, the stable bustled. Groomsmen and stable lads brushed by her, busy hauling hay bales and sloshing buckets. She scanned the space carefully, searching for Thomas, but he was nowhere in sight.

Fritz was immediately at her heels, scurrying about her feet, sniffing out the scents from the bucket.

"What are you doing?" came a gruff voice from behind.

She turned to find Master Telford with his arms crossed.

Calmly, she held up the bucket for Master Telford's suspicious eyes to see. "For the dog," she said.

Telford grunted. "That mutt eats better than most of us."

"I could give the scraps to the queen's horses, if you prefer," she offered meekly, looking curiously about.

Telford thought for a moment and then nodded. "Down there," he said, waving a hand at the opposite end of the stable. "Be quick about it. Then be on your way."

Beth bobbed a curtsy and swiftly headed to the stalls, Fritz following, not giving up on his meal.

Holbrook and Bayne's horses were as unmistakable as they were different.

The cleric's palfrey, a lean, dapple-gray gelding, dipped his head in a grain bucket, indifferent to her presence. Its tack was modest, but the brass cross affixed just beneath the cantle marked the horse's owner.

In the next stall, a strapping destrier, black as pitch, stamped its heavy hooves with impatience. Its tack was imposing, tooled with silver rivets, and a heavy embroidered cloth draped over its flanks bore the queen's colors of white, gold, and crimson. On one side, a Tudor rose; on the other, a golden cross. It was a warhorse, bred for power and fear—a beast suited for a man like Bayne.

Beth swallowed hard and unlatched the gate. She stepped in and approached slowly, hands steady though her heart raced. The horse's nostrils flared at her scent. "It's okay, boy. Easy now," she whispered.

She paused for a moment, letting him settle, then knelt and tipped over the bucket, dumping the scraps on the strewn hay.

The horse dropped his head, nibbling on the apple peels and rotting carrots as Beth moved to the girth strap. Her fingers worked quickly, slipping the knife from her pocket and sliding the blade under the leather. Holding her breath, she made two long cuts. The slits were deep but did not break through the strap. Just enough, she prayed, to give way during a hard gallop, enough time to slow them down, give her time to make a plan.

She pressed her hand to the destrier's neck. "Forgive me," she murmured.

Suddenly, raised voices drifted from the stable entrance.

"The servant girl, Beth! Where is she?" she heard Thomas shout. "Holbrook's men are searching for her."

Beth clasped her hand over her mouth.

"Brought a scrap bucket for the animals," came the reply from Telford. "She's down there."

Beth froze, then, without wasting another moment, she darted toward the tack room, calling for Fritz to come. She flung open the door, sprinting past the hay wagons and dung piles. The wind was biting. Her shawl flew wildly about as she clutched it tight, covering herself as best she could. There was no time to find warmer clothing. Her journey to Surrey had begun.

18

BETH

A light snow fell as Beth stumbled through the frozen woods. The road was dangerous, so she kept to the river, trusting it would lead her to Surrey.

By midday, the snowfall had thickened, hard and unrelenting. Her feet dragged with cold, and her hands were numb and raw. Fritz bounded ahead, zigzagging through the snow-covered reeds and brush, unfazed by the storm.

In the distance, the rattle of a carriage broke through the muffled hush of the woods. Beth turned toward the sound and struggled up the embankment, slipping on ice and roots. She no longer cared who the traveler was or what danger they might pose—only that they stopped to help her.

She stepped onto the road and raised a trembling hand.

The wagon wheels screeched to a halt.

Beth recognized the sturdy and practical low-riding wagon. Piled high with cloth and goods, it belonged to one of the draper merchants, carrying its wares to Surrey from the London markets. She had seen similar wagons at Abury Manor peddling bolts of wool, linen, and silk.

Snow blanketed the canvas cover, but she could just make out the three golden wheatsheaves with a bale of cloth on a blue background, the crest of the Draper's Guild.

An old man in a hooded cloak leaned over from the bench seat. The thick cowl framed a pair of wrinkled eyes brimming with concern.

"What are you doing out here in this foul weather, lass?" he exclaimed, scrambling down. He took her gently by the shoulders, studying her pale and wind-burned face. "Saints above, you're half frozen!"

Without another word, he shrugged off his sheepskin mantle, wrapped it around her shivering frame, and carefully helped her up into the wagon.

Fritz scrambled up after her, settling between the driver's boots with a satisfied shake.

Exhausted, Beth couldn't help but lean into the driver as the wheels jolted forward.

"Where am I taking you?" the man asked, letting her head rest on his arm.

"To Surrey," she murmured. ". . . To Agnes Montgomery."

Beth hardly remembered the journey to Surrey, nor the arms that gently laid her on the pallet bed in Gareth's family home. When she finally opened her eyes, she saw the worried crease of Agnes's brow as the woman knelt beside her.

Nestled near the hearth's warmth, Agnes propped Beth up with blankets as she spoon-fed her warm broth and tea steeped with mint leaves. The scents of earth and comfort filled the room—smoke, wool, and herbs. Agnes's touch was tender and her presence steady, like a mother tending a sick child.

"There's a God in heaven watching out for you, Beth, that's for certain," Agnes said, lifting another spoonful of broth to her lips. "I thought for sure you'd come down with a fever by now, but it's been a day, and no sign of it."

Rafe peeked out from behind his mother, his arms full of a squirming Fritz. "You're awake," he said with an impish grin.

"Yes," Beth answered. "And I'm happy to see you." She swallowed carefully, her voice still hoarse from the cold. "Any word from Gareth?" She knew not how long he planned to stay at Habington, but she hoped for his return soon.

Agnes paused, eyes fixed on the fire and shook her head.

The next day, Beth was strong enough to move about and help Agnes with simple chores. Keeping busy eased her worry about Gareth and Nicholas. She fed the hens, swept the hearth, and helped Rafe carry in wood as Fritz followed them dutifully, as he had done with Gareth.

The following morning, Beth finally heard the distant trot of hooves entering the yard. She looked up from the well, a full bucket in hand, but let it fall to the ground, seeing Gareth come into view, his shoulders slumped with exhaustion.

He slid from the Blackthorne's saddle and into her arms. There he held her—body trembling.

"You're back," she whispered. "You came back to me. What took you so long? Something has happened!"

Gareth didn't answer.

She pulled back, assessing him up and down. "Are you hurt?"

Gareth's dark eyes held a look of defeat, and her heart fluttered.

"They have him," Gareth told her. "The priest hunters took Nicholas. They arrived before dark and arrested him and two priests, hiding. Took them to London—to the Tower."

"No!" she breathed.

"I saw a way out through the guardhouse, but Nicholas refused to come when the cleric and his men stormed the manor. Said there were priests hidden there that needed his help." The words hitched in his throat. "I admired the man. As much as my father. But I left. Eager to get back to

Surrey—to you." He shook his head. "I should have stayed with him. Protected him!"

Beth reached for his hand. "Nicholas did what he wanted, despite the danger."

Gareth continued, as if not hearing her. "I traveled at night . . . in secret. Certain the queen's men were following me. But they weren't. It was Nicholas they wanted."

"Is there nothing that can be done?" Beth asked through her tears.

Gareth gently squeezed her hand. "I don't know."

She pulled her hand away. "That's not good enough! We must try, Gareth. Nicholas needs us! We'll go to London, find a way to see him. Help him escape!" she cried, her heart pounding.

Gareth looked away, his jaw clenched. "You make it sound easy. But what you say is impossible. I don't know London, and neither do you."

"I care little about what's possible or not," Beth said, her voice trembling. "I care only care that Nicholas waits chained behind a wall of stone to die."

She stepped closer, grasping his arm, her eyes shining with tears. "I'm going, Gareth. He needs us." Her voice dropped to a whisper. "You'll come, won't you?"

He pulled her into a tight embrace, and only then did her heartbeat calm. "Of course," he soothed. "We'll leave at dawn." He paused, raising his eyebrows. "There's something else, Beth."

She steadied herself. "What is it?"

"Bayne took a terrible fall from his horse. He was injured . . . badly."

Beth swallowed hard.

"They carried him in. Screaming the whole time. I doubt he'll walk again."

The ground blurred beneath her. "It was me," Beth said faintly. "Bayne's saddle . . . I crippled the girth with his own knife. I meant to detain them, to slow them down. Give you and Nicholas a chance to arrive safely." Her eyes flew open wide. "I never meant . . ." she stammered, but Gareth raised a hand to stop her.

"Did you forget what kind of man he was, Beth? He killed my father . . . and countless others."

She shook her head. "I'll never forget."

The North Downs Way was a well-trodden pilgrim path, heading east to London. Two riders on horseback would draw unwanted attention, so Beth and Gareth traveled on foot, each with a small satchel of bare essentials and a little food, just enough to last the three-day journey.

"It would have been easier on horseback," Gareth grumbled, trudging through the mud. "Blackthorne's seen worse mire than this."

"Easier, but more dangerous," Beth reminded him. She smiled to herself. Ever since she had told him Sir Charles had agreed to let him keep the horse, Gareth had grown more possessive of the animal, as if the gelding might vanish if left out of sight.

Centuries of foot traffic, livestock, and carts shaped the muddy, rutted holloway that wound through the fields and wooded hills. The ruts ran deep, and more than once Beth slipped on the slick mix of mud and frost.

An icy drizzle replaced the morning snow, and by mid-afternoon, as the first day of travel ended, they felt chilled to the bone.

Beth's pace slowed. Rain dripped from the sodden rim of her felted wool hat, and her cloak had soaked through. The old turn-shoes Agnes had lent her kept her feet dry enough but provided no warmth. Gareth did not fare any better. His cloak, heavy with rain, covered his shoulders like a burden, and every few steps, he cupped his hands to blow warm air into them.

"We need to find a place for the night," Beth said, stopping to catch her breath.

"The village of Shere is not far," Gareth replied, squinting at the fading daylight. "But we must hurry. These roads turn dangerous after dark."

An hour later, with daylight almost gone, they reached the edge of Shere Common. Beth looked around at the timber-framed cottages lining the lanes, their thatched roofs blackened by soot and age. Wagons creaked and lurched through the churned-up mire of the street, wheels half-sunk in mud. The thick scent of wet peat and burning wood hung in the air, mingling with the rank smell of damp earth and livestock.

A mangy cur shot out from beneath a cart and rushed at Beth, barking furiously. She stumbled back, nearly slipping into the muck, but caught her balance and hastily reached inside her cloak. Her fingers closed around the handle of a knife. She drew it and pointed the blade tip at the dog's bared teeth, hand shaking.

"Beth! No!" Gareth lunged forward. "Git!" he shouted, snatching up a stone and hurling it. The hound yelped and vanished into the mist that hovered low across the common.

Gareth's eyes dropped to the blade. "You still have Bayne's knife."

"I do. And I mean to keep it," she said, voice steady now. "There's no telling what lies ahead. I'll do what I must to protect myself."

"But I'll protect you," Gareth said, his eyes solemn.

She softened, just slightly. "I know you'll always keep me from harm." She held the knife between them before slipping it back into her pocket. "But I can protect us both now, too."

Gareth sighed, not wishing to argue. "I've a bit of coin," he said, revealing a small pouch tied to the belt under his cloak. "Not much, but enough for a bed at the inn."

Beth shook her head. "Best save it for London." She pointed at a church steeple rising dimly through the fog at the far end of the green. "Perhaps the parson will let us stay the night."

Gareth shrugged. "It's worth a try."

They made their way to the church. In the yard, a low wall outlined a cemetery, its stones mottled with moss and lichen. Crooked headstones marked the resting place of the dead, and the dark branches of the yew trees hung low on either side of the wrought-iron gate. Beth pulled her cloak tighter. Except for the wind in the branches, the air was silent.

At the church entrance, Gareth lifted the latch, and the heavy door creaked open. The church, once Catholic, still held its haunted remains. Faint outlines of saints and apostles long since scraped away and whitewashed over lingered like ghosts upon the plaster. The stained-glass windows remained, but the painted statues and gilded candle holders were gone, and the English Bible lay open on the lectern near the pulpit.

"May I help you?" a voice asked from behind.

Standing just inside the doorway was a vicar dressed in a black cassock and flat-topped cleric cap. Heavy eyelids and fleshy cheeks nearly hid his small, round eyes.

Gareth pulled off his cap and bowed his head. "My name is Gareth, and this is my . . . sister, Beth," he stammered. "We're on our way to London. We have kin in Southwark. They say there's work for those willing."

The vicar rubbed his chin. "Southwark, eh?"

"Yes, sir. Better than starving in the countryside," Beth added with a disarming smile.

"And you seek shelter?" the vicar asked.

"We do, sir. Just for the night," Beth said. "We'll be gone come morning."

The vicar looked at them, his eyes sharp under the heavy folds were unreadable. "I am Vicar Stephen Goodwin. You may call me Stephen, and you're welcome to stay the night in the parsonage kitchen. You'll be warm there and can dry your clothes." He held up a hand, assessing their exhausted faces. "But first, let's put some warm food into your stomachs."

The parsonage kitchen was modest, but orderly. A larder chest and grain barrel stood against the plastered stone beneath a small leaded glass window. The opposite wall held a cupboard. Its slightly ajar doors revealed pewter plates and cups. Bundles of rosemary and thyme dangled from exposed ceiling beams, and a rough-hewn trestle table with benches was centered in front of the fireplace. The flames crackled and popped, dancing beneath a simmering pot of stew. A black and orange striped cat lay curled on the warm hearth, purring contentedly.

While their clothes hung near the hearth to dry, Beth and Gareth sat at the table with Stephen, who offered them a meal of stew, pickled beets, and coarse bread.

The vicar ladled another helping of the thick broth into Beth's and Gareth's bowls. "Forgive the simplicity," he said with a wry smile. "My woman servant is away tending a sick aunt. I pray earnestly every day for her quick recovery. If I'm being honest, though, I miss her cooking more than I miss her company," he said with a hearty laugh.

Beth smiled, taking a sip of warm, spiced wine. "Do you often entertain travelers?" she asked.

"Aye, many travelers. Mostly pilgrims. Passing clergy. A few penny-pinching merchants too stingy for the inn. And sometimes travelers who enter the doors of St. James who keep their true intentions . . . close." He held her gaze, unblinking.

Gareth's goblet clanked against the table. "Sounds like you question our intentions," he said, his tone guarded.

Stephen rested his chin on his fist. "You're not the first souls to pass through Shere with burdens and secrets that weigh heavily on their hearts. And you are not the first to be creative with the truth." A knowing smile crossed his lips. "Neither of you is going to Southwark to sell wool at the market or fish on the docks. My niece lives in Southwark, and I'm told work is not easy to find these days." He poured more wine into Beth and Gareth's goblets. "And I sincerely doubt you're even siblings. So," he continued, "what is the real reason for your journey?" His voice was kind but held an underling warning that nothing but the truth would suffice.

Beth stared at her plate. "I don't know what to say except I'm sorry. Terribly sorry," she said, a flush rising to her cheeks. "We didn't mean to trick you. It's just . . ."

Gareth's eyes flicked from Beth to Stephen. "Trust is hard to come by," he finished.

"Indeed, it is," Stephen murmured. He paused for a long moment, eyes drifting up to the beams above as if searching for guidance. Then he said, "Are you Catholics fleeing persecution? Star-crossed lovers? You don't strike me as bandits."

"We are not Catholic," Beth answered.

Gareth shot her a sharp look, but she pressed on.

"There is someone very dear to us who practices the old faith. He's a good and righteous man who harmed no one. He's being held at the Tower. He needs our help."

Stephen's eyes widened. "The Tower! Well . . . not the answer I expected. To practice the old faith alone won't send a man to the Tower. Someone must've accused your friend of some grievous offence."

Beth's eyes flicked from Gareth to Stephen. "They arrested him for aiding priests," she answered, holding back the truth about the hidden priest holes, fearing the vicar's kindness might reach its limit sooner than his words suggested.

Gareth rose slightly from the bench. "Now you'll tell the sheriff and summon the queen's men!" His voice was hard, and his eyes flashed with anger.

Stephen raised his hand. "Calm yourself. Don't borrow trouble, lad, where there is none to be had." He nodded toward a shelf near the cupboard lined with worn books. "I may be the vicar of Saint James, but I am also a man of learning. A man of reason. A scholar of moral philosophy and an admirer of Sir Thomas More and the Humanist Movement."

Gareth eased back onto the bench. "You won't report us?"

Stephen shook his head.

"We can trust you?" Beth asked, her voice soft but her eyes watchful.

"As I trust you to keep my tolerant views in confidence."

Beth studied him. "So, you're against the Reformation."

Stephen held out his arms. "I am against extremism. I believe the Church must return to its roots, scripture, compassion, personal character." He smiled wryly. "There is plenty of reforming needed on both sides." He poured himself a little more wine and then asked with an easy tone, "Now, have either of you ever been to London before? My clerical training was at St. Paul's after my studies at Cambridge."

Gareth nodded. "A few times with my father when I was a boy. We traveled to a smithy to trade tools. I remember very little at all."

Stephen's eyes brightened. "A tradesman? Good. That may help. They stick together. You'll find no shortage of smiths in London. Look to the lanes about Smithfield, where the farriers labor, and east along the Minories near the Tower, where armorers and locksmiths ply their trade." His voice grew more serious. "But mind this, the Tower is heavily guarded. Don't be reckless, or impulsive, or you'll find yourselves in a cell next to your friend."

"We'll take care," Gareth answered.

Stephen stood, brushing his cassock of breadcrumbs. "Once you cross the river, you'll find the forges and merchants of Eastcheap. Press north to Smithfield and Billingsgate Market, then east along the lanes toward the Tower. You'll know it when you see it." He shook his head. "A towering fortress of stone and suffering. Not anything I would be eager to run to."

Beth's eyes drooped as she tried to stifle a yawn.

Stephen smiled and swallowed the rest of his wine. "I wish you well, and I'll pray for your safety and success, but for now." He stood and gestured to the blankets and bedding in the corner. "It is time for sleep."

Gareth inhaled deeply. "There is one more truth that needs to be told," he said. "You're right. Beth and I are not brother and sister. Beth is my . . ." His eyes locked onto hers. "Friend."

Stephen bent over and scooped up the cat. "I suspected as much," he replied, stroking the tabby's glossy coat. "As for tonight—since this is a house of God," his eyes twinkled as he wet his thumb and forefinger to snuff out the mantle candles, "let's pretend that you are."

19

BETH

They entered London late the following day, having gladly accepted the offer of a wool merchant from Shere to ride part of the way in his creaking wagon.

On foot, they traveled through Southwark along the bank of the Thames until crossing over the London Bridge into the district of Cheapside.

As they began their way to the other side of the river, Beth marveled at the massive gatehouse towers flanking the bridge's entrance. She had never seen a crossover like this one. London Bridge was an entity all its own. Tall buildings with shops lined the bridge on either side, and in some places the Thames was only visible through narrow gaps between the tightly built wooden structures.

The cobbled walkway was narrow and packed with carts, travelers, hawkers and animals, and the sound of rushing water below gave Beth a feeling of walking on air. Like its own small village, the bridge bustled with the commotion of sellers crying their wares. The smell of roasting meat wafted from the cookshops, along with the pungent stench of fish and boat tar.

The wealthy made their way through the crowd in fine carriages. Through the open-air windows, noble ladies pressed handkerchiefs against their faces.

Gareth pointed at a sign with a brightly painted pig. A brazier was set up beneath it to sell sausages. "Let's get one," he said with hungry eyes.

Beth's eyes danced with excitement. "Not now. We'll get food once we reach the city. We're almost there."

Gareth scrunched up his face and rubbed his stomach as if he were in pain, but Beth gave him a wry grin and pulled him along past the sausage stall.

On the other side of the bridge, Beth's head turned as if on a swivel as London rose before her, alive and breathing with aromas and clamor that assaulted the senses.

Timber-framed buildings lined the narrow streets, and centuries of boots and wagons had almost worn the cobblestones smooth. The hum of everyday life pressed against them from all sides. Dogs barked. Bells tolled. Children darted in between vendor carts and stalls.

A butcher flung a bucket of bloody water into the kennel, a watery canal of mud and waste that ran the length of the road, splashing Beth's skirts. She stumbled back, pulling her satchel tighter.

"Watch it!" Gareth shouted, but the man smirked and turned back to his shop.

Gareth's hand balled into a fist.

"No harm done," Beth said hastily, tugging his arm. "Let's keep moving."

The hawkers' cries—*fresh eels! hot pies! salted mackerel!*—pierced the air, and the stench of rotting food, dung, urine, and smoke churned her stomach.

Beth linked her arm with Gareth's, and they flowed along with the current of the busy street until Beth felt him pull away. She turned and saw him stopped in front of a food stall where a stout woman flipped hot pies with a knife; hot savory juices seeped from the flaky crust.

"Now can we eat?" he pleaded.

Unsure if her stomach was settled, Beth nodded anyway as Gareth pulled back his cloak, reaching for the coin bag tied to his belt.

"Careful with that," the pie woman said, eyeing the pouch. Her face was round and chubby, and, despite the cold, beads of sweat covered her upper lip and brow. "A cutpurse will nip that bag as easily as taking bread off a widow's table. Best keep it tucked inside your shirt."

"Thank you," Beth said as Gareth untied the pouch and stuffed it into his doublet.

They paid for two pies and continued their walk, eating as they went, Gareth finishing his in a few eager mouthfuls.

Soon they came upon a crowd gathered around two men fighting, their sleeves rolled to the elbows. One fighter was tall and wiry and quick on his feet, darting in with sharp jabs. The other man was shorter but heavyset and swung his arms with weighty, punishing blows. They held up their fists, shielding faces already bearing split lips and swollen cheeks, circling each other warily.

A man wove through the crowd collecting wagers and scratching down bets. Shouts rang out from all sides, urging on the fighters. The roar of the crowd swelled and receded like a wave.

Beth bit into her meat pie and looked away, not wanting to witness the spectacle.

Beside Gareth, a boy stood on his toes, straining his neck to watch.

"Care for a peek?" Gareth said to the child, who grinned and nodded eagerly.

Gareth swept the boy up onto his shoulders, and the lad clapped with delight, laughing as the fighters circled for another round.

Over her shoulder, Beth caught sight of a burly man, pressing in close, his eyes fixed not on the fight but on Gareth. Before she could speak, his hands shot forward and shoved Gareth hard into the throng. The boy tumbled from Gareth's shoulder into a tangle of legs. There was a flail of hands, an outcry of startled curses, and a shifting of feet as people regained their footing.

"Are you hurt?" Beth cried, helping Gareth up.

He didn't answer but threw open his cloak and patted frantically at his doublet, his face ashen. "It's gone, Beth! Our coin is gone!" he cried, his voice panicked.

"It can't be! I watched you hide it away!"

Gareth's hands fumbled with the opening of his doublet. The brass buttons that closed at the chest were undone. "I must have forgotten to button it," he said. "The fool that I am!"

Beth looked around. "The man and the child are gone!"

"The boy must have lifted it when I fell . . ."

Gareth's eyes searched wildly around. He grabbed Beth's hand and bobbed in and out of the crowd, desperately searching for the thieves before giving up.

"We're finished," he said with his hands on his knees, panting. "We can't stay without money. How will we eat? Where will we sleep?" He peered up at her, defeated.

She reached down, helping him to stand. "We have more to think about than ourselves. If it's coin we need, then we must earn it." She slipped her arm around his and pulled him away from the crowd, walking back down the thoroughfare.

"Where are we going?" he asked, still shaken.

"To find a blacksmith."

Beth and Gareth hurried from Cheapside to Tower Ward bound for the Tower of London. A cart driver had leaned from his seat as he'd pointed the way, warning them of the dangers lurking after dark.

"Nothing but cutthroats and whores once night comes," he had said, spitting on the cobbles.

They pressed on, following the lanes to Frenchurch Street, then down toward the Thames. The air thickened with the scent of tar and brine. Dockworkers and sailors shouted over the clatter of crates as ships bobbed at moorings, their rigging creaking against the pilings.

Rounding a bend, the Tower rose before them, its pale stone bleak against the darkening sky. Guards, traders, and craftsmen who served the garrison crowded the street. Merchants hawked wares from crooked, tightly packed timber-and-daub shops. The sound of a hammer pounding metal drew their attention. A few shops down was a blacksmith.

A signboard hung from a wrought-iron bracket with a crudely painted hammer and horseshoe. Double doors served as the entrance. One door left ajar showed off the ironware hanging on the walls.

Beth and Gareth stepped inside, and the warmth of the enormous forge set against the farthest wall enveloped them immediately. Beams and cross braces were dark with age and soot. In the middle of the workshop, an anvil stood on a stout oak block. Open crates filled with weapon parts stood against one wall. Tool racks held tongs, chisels, hammers, and swages of various sizes, all arranged with organized precision.

"What is it you need?" the blacksmith said, not looking up from the bolt he was forming. "Whatever it is, it won't get done until tomorrow. Got work orders in front of you to finish."

Beth and Gareth stood silent, unsure of how to answer.

"Well?" The blacksmith looked up. He was broad-shouldered with reddish hair that matched his full beard. The whites of his eyes appeared even whiter against his blackened, weathered face.

"Looking for work, sir. None to be had in Surrey, so I thought I'd try my hand here. I'm Gareth. My father taught me smithing from a tender age," he said with a slight hitch in his voice. He tipped his head toward Beth. "Beth here is a trained laundress." He eyed a pile of broken hinges and latches piled on the bench. "Looks like a successful man like yourself could use another pair of hands."

The blacksmith's dark eyes held a rueful glint. "If you call toiling every day with little rest 'successful' then, aye, I am the most fortunate man in London." He mopped his brow with a cloth. "I have no use for a laundress, but a smith . . . well, I may use you for a day or two. Name's Ulric. Come at dawn tomorrow."

"Please, sir," Beth broke in, "thieves stole our purse. We have no coin for food or a bed."

Ulric's lip curled. "Got nipped, did you?" He plunged the hot bolt into the water trough, sending a hiss of steam into the air. The corner of his mouth twitched. "You're not from here, that's plain."

"We're not asking for charity," Beth pressed. She looked away, her eyes focusing on the iron filings that littered the soot-blackened floor and the empty water pail near the door. "Let my friend work today. Enough to earn us a meal and a pallet at the inn . . . and I'll sweep your shop and fetch water."

"The day is almost done," Ulric replied, nodding at the darkening shadows outside.

"Which makes our situation even more urgent," Beth said, her eyes pleading. "We may be strangers, but we know of the danger night brings."

Ulric was quiet for a moment, rubbing his chin, then he said to Beth, "The broom is in the corner, but get water first from the barrel out back." He turned to Gareth. "There's a leather tabard hanging on the peg and gloves on the stool. I don't have a spare cap, so mind the sparks."

Gareth set to work at once, stoking the fire with charcoal until it glowed, the bellows whooshing with each pull. He passed Ulric the right tools before being asked, and Beth caught Ulric faintly smile, impressed by Gareth's speed and accuracy. Such mastery and knowledge of the forge usually came after many years of sweat and blistered hands.

Within an hour, Ulric's chilly demeanor thawed. He asked about Surrey, about the manor, and what it was like to live under its thumb.

Beth longed to know all about life in London, the markets and the people, but then another idea sparked.

"Business in Billingsgate must be brisk being so close to Cheapside, the docks . . . and the Tower," she remarked idly.

Ulric straightened from the anvil. "I craft shoes for the farriers and do a fair share for the shipbuilders." Then, after a pause, he said, "And, aye, the Tower keeps me busy as well."

Beth perked up. "What work?"

Ulric shrugged. "What do you mean, 'what work?' I don't understand, girl. Speak plain."

"For the Tower," she said, her eyes unflinching. "What goods do you forge?"

He sighed. "Lots of things. Sword guards, hilts, spearheads, and pommels for the garrison. For the kitchens . . . spits and fire irons. For the gaolers and the wardens, manacles, chains, and collars—and other devices too gruesome for delicate ears," he said, bringing the hammer down heavy.

"Devices of torture," Gareth said.

"Aye."

The raised voices of a fishmonger and a customer haggling over the price of mackerel drifted in from outside.

Ulric peered at them with curiosity, and he lowered his voice. "Why are you so interested in the Tower? Most folk scurry past the stone beast with closed eyes and ears, grateful to be on this side of those walls—unless, of course, someone close to them is on the inside."

He stopped short. A gleam shone in his eyes.

Beth stared at the man with eyes just as bright. "Care to swap a place to sleep and some bread for a story?"

It was late into the night when Beth and Gareth finished telling Ulric their tale. They gathered in the loft above the shop. The heat from the forge, always alive, seeped up through the floorboards and kept the cramped space warm. The loft, furnished with just a few stools, a battered table, and a feather mattress that served as a bed, was mainly used for storage. Sacks of charcoal slumped in one corner, and barrels of pitch and linseed oil were stacked haphazardly along the wall.

Beth sat on the soft mattress, back against the wall, sipping warm ale, while Gareth leaned on his elbows at the table. Ulric sat across from him, arms folded, a candle flickering between them. For a long moment, the blacksmith sat silent before speaking.

"You've got a dangerous undertaking," he said with a frown.

He fell silent again, the candlelight dancing over his weathered face. Beth and Gareth exchanged wary glances. It was madness to expect Ulric, a stranger, to risk his own life for them—for Nicholas.

"Reckless and foolish," he muttered at last. Then his eyes widened. "But not impossible." His thick fingers drummed against the tabletop. "I can get you inside, but once you're there, I can't keep you safe."

"Are you a papist sympathizer?" Beth asked hesitantly.

His eyes narrowed. "I sympathize with no religion. Not since Freida's passing." He leaned his arms on the table, staring at the single candle flame. "My wife favored the old faith. Tried to convince me of that way, too. By all that is good, she tried. But her life slipped away when she delivered our son. Her hand still gripped that wretched crucifix when they carried her out. The babe cold by her side." He looked up from the light. "I buried that damn cross with them. And I buried duty to any religion." His fist landed heavily on the table, making Beth jump. "Both sides can keep their God! He's no friend to me!"

"Yet, you'll help us?" Gareth asked.

"Aye, I'll help for Freida's sake. She would have wanted as much . . . kind-hearted as she was."

"We'll never be able to repay you," Beth said.

"Seeing a good man rescued from that cesspit is payment enough."

Gareth leaned in closer. "What's the plan?"

Ulric held up his hands. "I have something in mind, but it can wait until the morrow. Let me think about it and sleep." He rose and pulled two empty coal sacks from a pile in the corner, handing one to Beth and the other to Gareth. "Not used to having visitors. You'll have to make do with these. I'll sleep downstairs. No point in keeping you awake every time I stoke the fire." He took another empty sack from the pile and climbed down the ladder, bidding them goodnight.

Gareth blew out the candle, and through the gaps in the floorboards, a dull orange glow flickered from the banked coals downstairs, casting his shadow. He turned his face toward her and paused before spreading the coarse sack on the floor near her pallet.

"No," she whispered, "come here."

Gareth sank down on the mattress and settled in next to her, drawing her near to him in the crook of his arm. He smelled of cinder and smoke, the forge still clinging to him. She rested her head against his chest, listening to the steady rhythm of his heart. Ulric's rattling snore drifted up through the floorboards.

They lay in silence until Gareth said, "There was something comforting about working with Ulric today."

"You miss your father. I hear it in your voice."

He kissed the top of her head. "Tomorrow will be dangerous," he murmured.

"I know." The Tower rose in her thoughts—its thick walls and massive iron gates and portcullises guarding the entryways like jagged teeth. Archers patrolled the battlements, their eyes sharp, their bows ever at the ready. "Once back at Surrey, we'll find Peter. He can send Nicholas to John in Spain or smuggle him off to Scotland."

"That'll take some convincing," Gareth replied.

Beth's voice caught. "A stay in the Tower may be all it takes."

Gareth stroked her hair. "Stay here tomorrow. Ulric and I will go to the Tower." His voice was scarcely a whisper.

Beth pushed herself up on one elbow, the shadows catching the sharpness in her eyes. "No."

He cupped her cheek with a roughened palm. "I want to help Nicholas. I do. But I can't lose you."

She sank back down, letting his arm curl around her waist. "You won't. We'll look out for each other—like always."

20

GARETH

At daybreak, the sounds of Ulric sharpening his tools woke Gareth. Carefully, he slipped his arm out from under Beth, hoping to let her sleep longer, but her eyes drifted open and she smiled.

"Morning already?"

"Ulric's been awake for nearly an hour now," Gareth said, returning her smile.

Gareth helped Beth rise, and they made their way downstairs.

Ulric looked up from the knife he was filing and nodded toward the coins on the bench. "Fetch some boiled potatoes and cold fish from the market, and we'll break our fast."

"It's not right you payin' for our meal," Gareth said.

He shrugged, a grin tugging at his lips, his freshly washed face almost comely. "I'm not buying anything. You are. The coin is your wage for yesterday, and some extra for Beth." With a grunt, he hefted a crate full of blades, bolts, and locks and set it down near the door. "When you return, I'll tell you the plan for the Tower."

Gareth slipped the coins deep inside his doublet pocket and secured the buttons, glancing at Beth with a wry grin.

The two made their way to the dock. In the morning light, chimney smoke and a dim haze of fog off the Thames consumed the city. Seabirds circled above while the caw of crows perched high on the Tower walls pierced the chilly air.

They weaved their way through the tradesmen, merchants, and sailors preparing their ships and skiffs. Other folk mingled around the vendor carts, drawn by the smell of warm food. Women hawked pies steaming on wooden trays, boys shouted the price of oysters, and the hiss of frying eels rose above the din.

At a stall selling mackerel, they stopped.

"We'll take three," Beth said, pointing at the black, oily fish.

The old woman plucked three mackerel off the top of the pile and reached for a sack.

"Wait," Beth said, wrinkling her nose. "Pawning last week's catch as fresh, are we? Give us three from the barrel behind you."

The woman scowled but grudgingly handed over the fish from the new delivery.

"Well done," Gareth said with a grin as they continued on their way.

Beth's pretty lips curled into a smile. "You didn't think the woman would outfox me now, did you?"

A little farther down the lane, steam rising from an enormous cauldron caught Gareth's eye. "Potatoes," he said, pointing at the vendor's stall.

They had barely paid the seller when a rough hand clamped down on Gareth's shoulder.

Two sailors stood behind him, sizing him up. The man's hand moved to Gareth's arm, giving it a hard squeeze.

"Got muscles, this one," the shorter, stocky man said to his shipmate.

The taller, bearded man peered at him with eyes as sharp as gulls. He wore the queen's badge on his jerkin. "You've got the look of a fighting man. Come aboard with us and you'll never go hungry again."

Gareth stiffened. He knew the tales of men gone missing, pressed into the queen's service. "I am no sailor!" He shrugged off the man.

"You will be once you've tasted the salt air," the sharp-eyed man sneered and reached for Gareth's sleeve to drag him to a waiting boat.

Gareth twisted and pulled away, but the stocky sailor locked him in a grip from behind, holding his arms. Gareth raised his head in time to see Beth swing the sack of fish at the assailant. The blow caught the man in the face with a wet smack. He staggered back stunned, giving Gareth the opening to get away.

"God's wounds, woman!" the sailor roared, rubbing the welt on his cheek.

Fearlessly, she swung the sack again for another round, threatening the second sailor who stood watching with clenched fists.

"Touch him again and I'll gut your eyes out with a fish knife!" she cried, already fumbling for the blade in her skirt.

"No, Beth!" Gareth cried.

"C'mon," the man with the welt told the other sailor. "He's not worth the trouble. Besides, here comes the watchman."

The two men faded back into the crowd, cursing Beth as they went.

The watchman, armed with a lantern and a bell, approached. "What's all this about?"

"Two men were bothering the young lass, sir," Gareth said before Beth could speak. "I gave one a blow to the mouth. Now they're gone."

Beth's eyes widened, indignant.

"Get on your way then," the watchman replied, looking from Gareth to Beth with suspicion.

"Aye, sir," Gareth said, taking Beth's arm and pulling her along.

They had only gone a few steps when she jerked her arm away, her cheeks flushed.

"That's not what happened!" she hissed. "You nearly got yourself dragged into the Royal Navy if I hadn't stopped them!"

"And what if they'd hauled *you* off instead? I can handle myself, Beth! All you did was draw the watchman's attention! And that kind of attention is not what we need right now!" He realized he was shouting. Heads turned. Ears listened.

"Let's go," he said, dropping his voice. He tried to take Beth's hand, but she brushed him away, briskly moving a few paces ahead of him.

Back at Ulric's shop, Beth cooked the mackerel over the coals in silence. Gareth sat on a stool polishing a trivet near the tool rack, stealing glances as she moved the fish around on the skillet, wanting to speak, to apologize. He was angry with himself for not telling the watchman the truth.

A short time later, gathered around the workbench, Ulric swallowed the last of his meal and pulled a small clay pipe from his pocket, lighting it with a bit of straw. "Been making deliveries to the Tower for two years now. I know it well." After a few puffs, thin gray smoke circled his face. "Few folks get to see the royal apartments upstairs. I have. Fixed a few hanging hinges and floor grates up there." His eyes narrowed. "Beauchamp Tower holds high-ranking prisoners. The gentry and foreign nobles, that sort. You won't find your Nicholas there."

"Where, then?" Gareth asked.

"Given his crime? Most likely the White Tower—the dungeons, no doubt." He rose and tapped the pipe ash out on the edge of the forge. "There's no time to dally. We leave within the hour, delivering locks to the warders. We'll smuggle your friend out in an empty crate, and he'll ride undercover in the cart once—*if* we succeed." He eyed Gareth. "You'll be my apprentice. Follow my lead." Then to Beth he said, "You'll ride along as a laundress delivering clean bedding . . . just hitching a ride." He raised a bushy eyebrow. "Being a 'trained' laundress, you'll know the part, aye?"

Beth lifted her chin. "Well enough."

Outside, they loaded crates onto a cart, the largest big enough to hold a man. An old mule, tied and harnessed, waited. Ulric dropped a heavy sack, stuffed with old rags meant to fool the guards into thinking it was clean washing, onto the ground.

Beth bent to lift it, straining with the weight. Gareth stepped forward to help.

"I don't need your help," she snapped, shooting him a glare before storming back into the shop.

Ulric heaved another crate into the cart and shook his head. "God's sake, lad. What did you do to anger the girl?"

Gareth brushed the damp hair from his brow. "Let my pride get the better of me," he muttered. "As always."

21

BETH

The trip to the Tower of London was not far, but the road was thick with merchants, peddlers, and beggars trailing behind with outstretched hands. Every few yards, the cart jolted to a stop to avoid pedestrians and other wagons. Ulric flicked the reins and cursed under his breath.

Beth and Gareth rode at the end of the cart, their feet dangling above the mired road.

Beth's eyes wandered upriver to London Bridge, its stone arches spanning the Thames like a humped-back serpent. The crooked houses piled on top leaned and tilted as if they might topple into the water.

At last, the road widened as they reached Tower Hill.

Ulric turned his head. "That's where they carry out executions," he called back solemnly, nodding toward a raised yard outside the stone walls.

The space was empty save for a wooden platform near the stone wall with several steps leading up its side.

Beth imagined throngs of common folk craning for a view, shouting and jeering while some poor soul awaited death. Her mind at once went to Nicholas and how he must be suffering within these same walls. Her chest tightened at the grim reminder of the queen's reach.

"It's as horrid as everyone says it is," Gareth said, turning his face away.

They were his first words since leaving Ulric's shop. Beth's anger was not so easily pacified. She regretted her sharpness on the dock, but he had wronged her, and it stung. Puffing himself up to the watchman had only revealed his immaturity. He should have been grateful for her intervention, not scornful. Still, their goal was the same, and the thought softened her anger.

"All the more reason to find Nicholas quickly," she answered.

But Gareth wasn't listening. His gaze was locked on something else.

Beth turned. Across from the scaffold, four men swung from a tall crossbeam, their necks twisted in nooses. The corpses swayed faintly in the breeze, faces blackened and tongues protruding. A cloud of flies buzzed about them.

She inhaled sharply, the rotting stench reaching her before she could look away. The fish and potatoes rose in her throat. She pressed her hand to her mouth, but it was too late. Leaning over the cart's edge, she retched violently onto the passing cobbles as the cart rolled past.

Gareth reached for her hand, and she let it rest in his.

A few moments later, the cart rumbled onto a short bridge spanning a moat and came to a halt behind several wagons forming a line. At the end of the bridge, a watchman's gate awaited. A portcullis hung above the arched entrance, ready to crash down to secure the Tower against an enemy.

Ulric turned to them, his voice low. "Byward Gate," he said. "There'll be questions and an inspection. Be ready."

Beth twisted her hands nervously as Gareth stood, pulling the canvases off the crates.

She glanced farther down the curtain wall to another gate down at the water's edge. A skiff with three men drifted toward the entrance. The oars sliced slowly through the dark brown water until the boat scraped against the stone landing. As the men stood, Beth saw the flash of the queen's colors on two of them. The third wore a torn nobleman's doublet, his hands bound behind his back, his head bowed as if the weight of the Tower already pressed upon his shoulders. The guards roughly helped the prisoner out of the boat and up the stone steps before disappearing beneath the archway into the shadow.

"Traitor's gate . . ." Beth murmured. Its infamy was legendary, and she wondered if Nicholas, too, had been swallowed by the same shadow.

"It is said that those who enter there never come out again," Gareth whispered, his eyes wide.

The cart rolled on, taking its turn at the front of the line. Two guards in breastplates stood sentry on either side of the entrance while another guard approached the cart, his halberd gleaming despite the morning fog. Sharp eyes peered up from his weather-beaten face as he rapped the cart's wheel with the butt of his weapon, a dull thud echoing against the wood.

"State your business," he barked at Ulric.

"Blacksmith from Billingsgate Market. My apprentice and I are delivering locks and hinges to the warders," Ulric replied, his voice steady as iron.

The guard's gaze slid past Gareth and fixed on Beth. "What about her?" the man said, tracing Beth's form with his eyes. "She's like no blacksmith I've ever seen."

"A laundress," Ulric replied evenly, not missing a beat. "Twisted her foot leaving the market. Just giving her a ride."

The guard lifted one crate's lid and then lowered it. Satisfied, he stepped closer to Beth, his eyes narrowing on the bulging sack at her side. Her heart pounded.

"Open it," he said with a curled lip.

Beth's mouth went dry, her heart hammering even harder against her chest. There was no mistaking dirty rags for clean washing.

He leaned closer, his breath smelling of ale. "Didn't you hear me, girl? Open it!"

Ulric swung around on the bench. "Are you blind, man? That's washing. If you want to paw through a woman's clean linens, be my guest. But don't delay the warders' ironwork over a woman's rags," he said.

The man paused for a moment, perhaps considering the weight of Ulric's words and the wrath of the warders.

At last, he grunted, slapping the mule's flank. "Move on," he growled.

The cart jolted forward. Beth released the breath she'd been holding. Her pulse throbbed in her temple as and she felt the eyes of the guard follow her.

***

The cart rumbled into the outer ward of the Tower, its wheels clattering past other carts loaded with firewood and food. A wide courtyard spread before them, bound by high curtain walls and watchful towers. Beyond another set of walls hemmed in the inner ward, a place that was said to be both a palace and a prison.

Yeomen in bright Tudor livery drilled in neat formations, while warders, servants carrying baskets, and kitchen boys with pails and barrels hurried in every direction.

Chickens darted between wagons, chased by lean dogs, and the stench of dung and kitchen smoke hung in the air, a reminder that the place was not only a prison but a garrison, mint, armory, and noble lodging.

Beth clutched the edge of the cart, imagining a prisoner delivered into such bustling chaos only to be thrown into the pitch of darkness and a silent cell. Several smaller towers ringed the inner ward. Slate roofs capped their square turrets. In the center, the White Tower, with its massive stone bulk, rose like a master over his servants.

The cart creaked forward into the narrow-arched gate of the inner wards. The walls pressed close, damp with centuries of smoke and torchlight. Gareth turned to her, his brow creased with worry. Beth slipped her hand in his for a moment, careful not to be seen. Fortune had been with them at the first crossing, and she could only pray for deliverance again.

Two yeomen planted their halberds to block the way. Between them stood a sergeant; his dark eyes flicked from one face to another from beneath the rim of his morion helmet.

"Your business?" the sergeant ordered, his voice echoing in the vaulted passage.

"Locks and hinges for the warders. Some repair work, too," Ulric said, his voice unwavering. "Billingsgate smithy. You've seen me before."

The sergeant took a step closer. "What about her?" he asked, eyeing Beth.

She breathed deeply and lowered her eyes, acting the part of a lowly servant.

"Laundress for the lieutenant," Ulric said just as steadily.

The sergeant reached out and raised Beth's chin with his gloved finger, his eyes tracing the lines of her face. "Is that what we're calling wenches now?" he said with a smirk, pulling his hand away. "You'll not wander in the inner ward. Straight to your work and back out. Understood? That goes for you too, *laundress*."

"Aye, sir," Ulric answered, and Beth gave a dutiful nod.

The man raised two fingers, and the yeomen moved their halberds aside. Ulric clucked his tongue, and the mule pulled forward.

Unlike in the outer ward, the air here was eerily hushed, broken only by the harsh caw of crows and the muffled clink of keys disturbing the silence. The White Tower loomed at its center. Its battlements bristled with guards following every movement below.

They stopped again outside a wooden entryway bound in iron. Ulric swung down from the bench and rapped hard on the door three times.

Boot steps echoed across the cobblestones made Beth turn. At the far end of the curtain wall, two yeomen dragged a prisoner between them, his arms secured in their grip. His doublet was torn. His head was bowed. It was the prisoner from Traitor's Gate, but there was something familiar in the rhythm of his step that seized Beth's attention.

Gareth leaned close. "It's Lord Charles," he whispered.

Beth's throat tightened. "Holbrook has withdrawn his promise of leniency," she breathed, her words tumbling fast.

The guards moved quickly past them, heading towards another smaller tower. Heavy bruises marked Lord Charles's face, and blood dripped from his split lip.

"Taking the poor bastard to Beauchamp Tower," Ulric said under his breath, watching Charles go by. "Nobles are held there once they're punished or broken."

Beth and Gareth looked away, not wanting to be seen. Charles stumbled past, unaware. They heard the scrape of iron as the gate of the Beauchamp Tower swung open. Charles lifted his face to the gray sky before they shoved him inside.

"He's no poor bastard," Gareth told Ulric. His voice was thick with anger, and his fists curled at his sides. "He told the queen's men everything they wanted to know about Nicholas and the hidden priest hole. Thought it'd be an easy way out. Looks like that plan didn't fare so well for him."

"It's because of him that Nicholas is here," Beth added just as angrily, though her stomach still soured at the sight of Charles stumbling like a broken man.

"Lord or not, they all rot the same once the Tower swallows them," Ulric replied, shaking his head. His eyes darted to the guards on the wall. "But sitting and staring with mouths hanging only draws unwanted attention. Gareth, start unloading the crates. Beth, leave the sack and join him." He gave her a sly grin, but his eyes held no mirth. "You're no longer a laundress or a wench but my helper."

Ulric pounded on the door again, and a warder appeared. His jerkin was worn, and a leather cap failed to cover a bald crown. He listened with a pinched face as Ulric explained their purpose.

"Come ahead, then," the man said, waving them in. "The ironmongery is in the lower chambers. You'll be shown down."

"Don't need an escort. Been down those god-forsaken steps many times," Ulric said. "Was delayed quite a bit this morning. Now I'm late."

The warder's brows furrowed, squinting a look at Beth and Gareth. His mouth opened to protest, but Ulric hoisted a crate by the rope handles, shouldering his way past as if the matter was already settled. Beth and Gareth hurried to slide the crate for Nicholas off the cart, each grabbing a metal handle, and followed behind. The warder grunted and walked back into the shadows, mumbling as he went.

They followed a dim hallway lit by torches to a cavernous room used as an armory and storage. Racks of pikes and barrels of powder stood along the walls. A broad spiral stair of worn stone curled up into darkness, while another narrower stair led down into the earth.

"That way," Ulric said, nodding toward the narrow steps.

They moved slowly, taking care not to slip on the slimy stones. Moisture from the Thames seeped through the walls. The smell of damp straw and rotting wood grew stronger the lower they went until Beth shivered, her breath cold in her chest.

At the bottom, the passage widened into a corridor with barred cells on either side. Groans of captives drifted in the air, broken by muffled screams from deep in the dark. Ulric glanced at Gareth and tilted his head toward the prisoners. Gareth gave him a grim nod, but Beth, stumbling on an uneven stone, drew the eye of a yeoman standing guard.

"No escort?" the soldier barked, his eyes narrowing.

Ulric gave a careless shrug. "Wasn't offered one," he lied.

The yeoman stepped forward, his eyes flashing with indignation. "Well, you have one now. Why are you here?"

"Delivering bars, chains, and hinges—and there's a lock to repair. Bolt keeps jamming."

"Which cell?"

"Not sure. Warder wasn't sure himself. Gaoler left that part out, but I'll know just by the rattle," Ulric said, shifting the crate in his arms. "But I can't hold this load any longer." He put the crate down against a wall. Beth watched as he deftly untied his tool roll from his belt and slipped it inside the crate. "I'll fix the lock first and make the delivery on the way out. Where do we start?"

The yeoman looked confused but then nodded. "This way." His boots struck the stones hard as he strode off, forcing them to keep up.

He stopped at the first row of cells and waited. Iron rings and shackles were fixed into the walls, ceilings, and floors. Inside the first cage, a young man in a tattered tunic lay on a pile of filthy straw, not moving. Open sores and lashes covered his legs and arms.

Ulric shook the bars hard and gave Beth a sideways glance. She responded with a slight shake of her head. "Not this one," he called over his shoulder to the yeoman.

They moved from cell to cell, Beth and Ulric, silently communicating with only a glance and a head shake, until they stopped at a cell near the end. Beth peered inside and drew a quick breath, her face ashen.

Nicholas sat on the stone floor against the wall, spectacles gone, his legs splayed out awkwardly in front of him. Beth cleared her throat, her eyes piercing into Ulric, who gave the bars a quick shake.

"This one," he said to the yeoman.

The man rolled his eyes. "Always the farthest one."

Ulric crouched, surveying the lock. "Get my tool roll, boy. And hand me a hammer and chisel. And you," he said, pointing at Beth, "open that crate and find another lock with a bolt. Be quick about it. The yeoman has other things to do."

Beth opened the crate, fighting the urge to speak to Nicholas. Gareth looked around confused.

"There's . . . no tool roll, sir," he stammered.

Ulric looked up with a snarl. "Then you left it behind in the other crate, you fool! Fetch it now, boy!"

The yeoman stiffened. "I'll go with you. You can't be wandering down here alone."

Ulric looked up with a frown. "Fine idea. This boy can't find his own arse with a map and a torch!"

The man muttered under his breath, motioning sharply for Gareth to follow. Their boots echoed on the flagstones as they disappeared around the bend of the passage.

Beth grasped the bars, pressing her face between them. "Nicholas," she whispered.

Nicholas lifted his head and squinted toward her. "Beth?" he answered, his voice weak and raspy. "Is it really you?"

"Yes, I'm here—with Gareth and Ulric, a trusted friend. We're going to get you out."

The cell fell silent. Only the drip of water and the muffled weeping from another prisoner filled the space between them.

"Oh, sweet girl," he said at last, his gaze dropping to his twisted limbs. "I won't be going anywhere. My legs and arms are no longer at my command."

Ulric's jaw tightened. "They've put him to the rack," he said. "The bastards!" His voice was low but edged with fury.

Beth's mouth went dry. Her fingers tightened around the bars. "Then we'll carry him," she shot back, her voice rising.

"Not past the guards. Not past the gate," Ulric replied. "We won't make ten steps before they hear him cry out."

Nicholas let out a pained laugh. "She means to smuggle me out like a sack of barley. Your friend is right, Beth. I am touched by your courage—and your heart—but you've chosen too heavy a burden."

Beth blinked back tears. "You are no burden! You are family!" she told him fiercely.

"As I will always be," he whispered. "But this is my path now. My journey here is nearly done . . ." He drew a rattled breath. "And what a journey it has been."

Ulric rested a heavy hand on her shoulder and bent near to her. "There is nothing to be done. Taking him now would be cruel, and we'd all end up in the cell beside him. *You must let him go.*" He gave her shoulder a gentle squeeze. "Soon, he'll be free of his earthly bondage. Free from pain," he finished.

Tears flowed down her cheeks as she released her grip on the bars. "I failed you."

"You've failed no one," Nicholas said faintly. "Not you, nor Gareth. An act of love can never fail . . . and what you all have done will never be forgotten."

The faint sound of boot steps grew louder. Gareth and the yeoman rounded the bend in the corridor, the tool roll in Gareth's hand.

Beth hastily swiped the tears away with the back of her hand. Ulric straightened, his expression returning to that of an irritated taskmaster.

"At last!" he growled, snatching the tool roll from Gareth's hand. "Do you know how much time you've wasted?"

Beth, still trembling, bent and rummaged through the crate. She found the lock and bolt and handed them to Ulric, who began replacing Nicholas's lock, his hands working swiftly.

Gareth moved closer to Beth, his eyes fixed on Nicholas. "What is to be done?" he asked under his breath.

She stared back, her eyes pricked with fresh tears. "Nothing. It's over. He cannot walk. They've broken him," she whispered back, her voice catching in her throat.

Gareth drew a deep breath and lowered his head, staring at the cold stones beneath him.

The yeoman banged his torch against the wall. "What are you two mumbling about?" he barked, his eyes narrowing.

"Probably complaining about the wages they'll be docked for their stupidity!" Ulric sneered. "I'm nearly done. Make yourself useful." He tossed the hammer to Gareth. "Put that away."

Ulric finished his work, and they prepared to leave. Gareth tied Ulric's tool roll and handed it to Beth to put in the crate.

Lifting the lid, she turned to Nicholas one last time. He met her gaze with the faintest smile; his eyes shone with love and gratitude as he mouthed a single word—*Go*.

22

BETH

Winter's bitter grip had finally loosened, giving way to spring's promise of new life.

Primrose, violets, and bluebells bloomed along the woodland paths. Birdsong filled the air once more, and farmers welcomed the birth of calves and downy-coated lambs into their folds.

Beth pulled the garden hoe through the soft soil in Agnes's kitchen garden, preparing rows for peas, leeks, and spring herbs.

Many weeks had passed since Nicholas's failed rescue, and Beth's future lay before her still uncertain, a path unwilling to oblige her forward or backwards.

Life meandered on with all its daily twists and turns, but the memory of Nicholas and his martyrdom stood steady in her mind and heavy on her heart, unmoving, like a stream dammed with stones.

Dreams of Nicholas with torn limbs and an unbroken spirit haunted her sleep. If only they had arrived at the Tower sooner and whisked him away to Spain, he'd be alive and whole.

Gareth had said little to her about Nicholas, choosing instead to bear the pain alone. The choice left her with little solace, suffocating her with a silent grief.

Beth breathed in the loamy scent of earth and managed a smile as Rafe came bounding towards her, full of youthful energy.

"There's a man!" Rafe blurted, breathless. "In the barn, talking to Gareth. He told me to fetch you—quick!"

Beth dropped the hoe, gathered her skirts, and hurried to the barn across the yard, fearful the queen's men had returned to the village.

Rushing inside, she stopped short. Her eyes widened.

"Peter?" she gasped.

"Thought you'd be happier to see me," he said, grinning.

Beth laughed and threw her arms around him. "Is all well? Is John in Spain? Why didn't you go with him?"

"Slow down!" he said, raising a hand. "Word came last week. John is safe—under King Philip's protection, no less." He shook his head. "No, I didn't go with him. I've watched over that boy his whole life. It's time I got on with mine."

He glanced back at Gareth. "I was just asking if he could use another pair of hands at the smithy."

"Business is good," Gareth replied with a rare smile. "The help would be welcome."

"It's settled then," Peter said, then paused. His voice softened. "I heard about Nicholas."

Beth nodded, feeling a familiar ache tightening in her chest. "A martyr's death," she answered quietly.

"Indeed," Peter murmured. "Never gave up a single priest hole. Or priest."

"It was a gift to see him one last time," Gareth added softly. "Despite our failure."

"Nay," Peter replied. "You did all that could be done. It is what good folk do—help one another, no matter the odds. Nothing else could have been done for Nicholas. He knew that too. He accepted his fate as he accepted his life's work—with grace." He looked between them, his gaze steady. "Now you must do the same." After a long moment, he leaned closer, his voice low. "Word is Bayne no longer travels with Holbrook. Can barely walk after that fall."

Beth's tearful eyes flicked between the two men, but she said nothing. Her part would remain a secret between her and Gareth.

"And what of Kat?" she asked. "Did she find help among the womenfolk?"

"Aye, they welcomed the girl with open hearts. I stayed a while just to be sure," Peter replied. "How does she fare?" He shrugged. "I can't say. That kind of pain . . . it runs deep."

Beth nodded. "Perhaps you'll take me there sometime? I'd like to see her."

Peter smiled. "Of course."

Gareth scraped the sole of his boot on the packed earth floor. "What will become of the manor now that Lord Charles rots in the Tower?"

"Lady Eleanore won't be a ladyship for long, I fear," Peter replied

"She's lucky not to be alongside her husband in chains," Gareth muttered.

Beth touched his arm. "Don't judge too harshly. She meant no harm. The blame shouldn't rest on her shoulders for her husband's sins."

Peter rubbed his chin. "She'll be forced to rely on the charity of kin, I reckon."

"Still better than the Tower," Gareth replied bitterly. "Still better than what they did to Nicholas . . ." He turned to Beth; tears flooded his eyes as his face crumbled under the weight of all he'd kept locked away.

She rushed to him and held him as the sobs overtook him.

Peter moved closer and rested a hand on Gareth's shoulder. "You and Beth stood up to the oppressors," he said, his voice low, but firm. "To have done nothing would've been worse. Don't lament the past. Nicholas's love is not lost. Neither is his mission. The priest holes will still be built—though I pray the day will come when they won't be needed."

Gareth pulled Beth away and held her at arm's length, searching her eyes. "We did our best, you and I, did we not?"

Beth blinked back tears with a sudden knowing. "We did," she answered firmly, letting the grief settle between them into a silent, sacred place. "Peter is right. I still feel Nicholas in my heart—and always will."

Blackthorne whinnied from his stall and bobbed his head.

Peter let out a slight cough. "I see you've got that fine gelding now," he said, offering a handful of straw to Blackthorne.

Overhearing Peter from the pen of newborn piglets, Rafe rushed to Gareth. "Is Blackthorne really yours now?" he asked, looking up at his brother with wide eyes.

Gareth drew his sleeve across his eyes. "He's *ours*," he said, tousling his younger brother's hair. "You'll help me care for him, won't you, Rafe?"

"Of course!" came Rafe's quick answer.

"Then fetch him some more hay and water," Gareth teased, his wet eyes brightening.

That evening, Peter stayed and shared a simple meal of pottage and fresh bread with them. Agnes, grateful for the company, moved through the old cottage with renewed purpose. The fire crackled. Laughter returned. And the home seemed to breathe again.

Agnes set a pitcher of ale on the table and eased onto the bench. "Have you asked her yet?" she said with a knowing smile at her eldest son.

Beth looked at Gareth in confusion.

Gareth gave his mother a sheepish grin and turned to Beth. "What my mother means is we want you to stay here with us." His eyes were steady, his tone hopeful. "What I really mean is . . . I want you to stay here with me."

Beth's smile bloomed as she reached for his hand across the table.

She was home. And there was love.

Enough to last a lifetime.

The end

AUTHOR NOTE

I first stumbled upon the fascinating life of Saint Nicholas Owen while watching a historic documentary about Elizabethan England.

As described in the book, Nicholas was a devout Catholic and skilled carpenter who risked—and ultimately gave—his life to protect persecuted priests and to build secret places known as "priest holes" to hide them.

Nicholas Owen built these ingeniously concealed spaces across the country, including locations such as Hindlip Hall, Baddesley Clinton, and Harvington Hall. Many priest holes were so well hidden that they remained undiscovered for centuries. Priest holes are still being revealed today.

Physically, Nicholas was not the strapping, cliche carpenter one typically thinks of for such extraordinary undertakings. He was born with a malformed leg, suffered from a hernia, and was relatively small in stature. These physical afflictions made his life's work and contribution to history even more remarkable and, in my opinion, heroic.

Following his arrest in 1606, they brutally tortured him in the Tower of London, and he died under interrogation. Through it all, he never divulged the location of any priest hole or priest.

In 1970, Nicholas Owen was canonized as one of the Forty Martyrs of England and Wales by Pope Paul VI. He is the patron saint of illusionists and escapologists.

– If you enjoyed *Of Heaven and Hellfire*, I would be grateful if you'd consider leaving me a review on Amazon and Goodreads. Also, I invite you to check out my debut novel, *Divinity Undone*, which won a 2025 Next Generation Indie Books Finalist Award in the pre-1900s historical fiction category, and, as always, thank you. Time is precious, and I appreciate you lending me some of yours.

DISCUSSION GUIDE

1. Beth, Gareth, and others risk their lives to help Nicholas and the Sheffields hide John, despite not being Catholic. Do you think they made the right choice? Would you have chosen differently in their place?

2. Lady Eleanore, despite her position, is vulnerable once Lord Charles is imprisoned. What does her fate say about women's limited choices in Tudor society?

3. How does Beth evolve from a servant girl to someone who actively shapes her own destiny? Which moments best reveal her growth in courage and conviction?

4. Sir Richard Bayne and Reverend Holbrook both

make potent antagonists. If you had to face one of them in real life, which one would you find more intimidating?

5. Beth, Lady Eleanore, Kat, and Agnes each face their own limitations and dangers as women in Elizabethan England. How do they navigate their lack of power?

6. Sir Richard Bayne and Reverend Holbrook wield their authority in different ways. Which do you think is more dangerous, the brute force of Bayne or the calculated zeal of Holbrook?

7. The novel is set against the backdrop of Elizabeth's penal laws and religious divisions. Did the historical backdrop enhance the story for you? What surprised you most about daily life in Tudor England as shown in the novel? Would you survive in that world?

8. Ulric risks his position and safety to help Beth and Gareth. Why do you think he chose to help them? What does loyalty mean in a time when trust could cost you your life?

9. The novel concludes with Beth finding "home" not just in a place, but in love and a sense of

belonging. How do different characters define home throughout the story, and how does that meaning shift?

10. If the book were adapted into a film or series, who would you cast as Beth, Gareth, Nicholas, and Bayne?

www.ingramcontent.com/pod-product-compliance
Lightning Source LLC
Chambersburg PA
CBHW030106260626
47156CB00008B/2538